What people are saying ab[illegible]

This Is All He [illegible]

A tender story about human [illegible] with compassion.
Jenny Downham, award winning novelist, author of *Before I die, You against me,* and *Unbecoming*

This story collection celebrates the joyful intimacy of being alive. Anne Egseth writes from her heart and her words simply flow. This book is a treasure!
Johanna Baldwin, writer, producer and author of the Dr. Raymond Moody inspired novel, *All (Wo)men Desire to Know*

This lovely book is delightful, funny, and at the same time genuinely profound. Wisdom runs through the narrative like a vein of gold through quartz, evoking an inner sense and capacity which is both real and desperately needed in our troubled, heedless times. An authentic voice, a story which lingers in the mind like a fragrance.
Lucy Oliver, *The Meditator's Guidebook*

In *This Is All He Asks of You*, author Anne Egseth unpretentiously weaves symbols and images together to create an alluring, luminous tale of a young woman's search for understanding and meaning. It is an all at once haunting and captivating reflection on relationship, not just with others but with the self. Written in a classic, quiet Scandinavian style, it distills great wisdom and the redemptive energies of grace and acceptance, so urgently needed in our world today.
Dielle Ciesco, author of *The Unknown Mother: A Magical Walk with the Goddess of Sound*
Seldom have I read such an extraordinary and thought provoking

tale as Anne Egseth's debut novel, *This Is All He Asks of You.*

This is an enchanting and imaginative story that will engage anyone of any age, a book that drew me in so completely that I just couldn't put it down.
Veryan Williams Wynn, author of *The Spirit Trap*

A poignant tale of despair and hope, traced through the eyes of a young girl, *This Is All He Asks of You* delves deep into the psyche of 12-year-old Luna, who is somewhat "different" or so she believes, to her peers and friends. This warm and complex story of tears, laughter, friendship and love, explores the devastation that so often occurs when sensitive souls have to deny the very core of their being. Is Luna the only one who understands the light? Or, as we grow, do too many of us lose it somewhere along the way?
Ashley Costin, author of *Emajen*

This Is All He Asks of You is as an evocative account of a young woman's struggles to reclaim what we've all lost "the day the light went out" as I've ever read. You will never forget Luna, and hopefully she will help you reclaim that light as well.
John Nelson, author of *The Miracle of Anna*

This is a simple, yet deeply moving story about the power of love and light in our lives. Spiritual at heart and authentic in form; this is a slow-paced account of the importance of our connection to the natural world and to each other.
Anne Synnøve Simensen, author of *The Woman behind the Nobel Peace Prize: Bertha von Suttner and Alfred Nobel*

This Is All He Asks of You is a very poetic and intriguing book that will make you mull over where your own life has taken you.
B.R. Wilkerson, author and winner of the 2018 NY Big Book Award

This Is All He Asks of You

This Is All He Asks of You

Anne Egseth

Winchester, UK
Washington, USA

First published by Roundfire Books, 2020
Roundfire Books is an imprint of John Hunt Publishing Ltd., No. 3 East St., Alresford,
Hampshire SO24 9EE, UK
office@jhpbooks.com
www.johnhuntpublishing.com
www.roundfire-books.com

For distributor details and how to order please visit the 'Ordering' section on our website.

ISBN: 978 1 78904 353 2
978 1 78904 354 9 (ebook)
Library of Congress Control Number: 2019937726

A CIP catalogue record for this book is available from the British Library.

Design: Stuart Davies

UK: Printed and bound by CPI Group (UK) Ltd, Croydon, CR0 4YY
US: Printed and bound by Thomson-Shore, 7300 West Joy Road, Dexter, MI 48130

Contents

For Olivia

Is not this, perhaps the secret of every true and great mystery, that it is simple? (...) Proclaimed, it were but a word; kept silent it is being. And a miracle too, in the sense that being with all its paradoxes is miraculous.
C. Kerenyi, *Introduction to a Science of Mythology*

PART I

The Parcel

Tromsø, Norway, November 2018

For three months now, instead of studying for my exams, I have been sitting at my white desk, alternating between staring at the ghostly landscape outside and sifting through the words of a twelve-year-old me.

Now that the words are here, they fill the space and crowd my head as I look out of the window. The snow is black. It was pure and soft, and now it is hard, dirty and icy. I know that this grainy, black snow will line the streets outside for many months. Slowly, I will forget that warmth and sun and spring are possible. Every year, I forget. And then suddenly, as if out of nowhere, the ice will melt, the mud will stick to my shoes, and new life will be revealed. You should know this, as you grew up here as well. Or have you forgotten what it is like when the sun goes away for months on end, and the short glimmer of light at noon is too weak to carry the slightest hope of spring?

The words came in a parcel that arrived on my doorstep a while ago. A shoe-box filled with letters, poems, homework: snapshots of a girl I had forgotten, from a time when miracles could coexist with mashed potatoes, gray asphalt and science homework. It was mailed by an old friend, who kept it in his attic for ten years. It traveled across the ocean, all the way from Washington, D.C. to Tromsø. I didn't remember that I had given it to him, or even that it ever existed.

I look at the crumpled papers as I transform the wiry and scattered handwriting of my younger self into the orderly, black rows of signs on my computer. This is my attempt to create chronology, continuity and coherence out of a time I had wiped out of my memory. I don't claim this is exactly what it was; this is me weaving a net of words, trying to catch this elusive, slippery voice from the past. I am following the thread back to a frozen girl buried deep inside my body; a twelve-year-old who disappeared the day the light went out. As I write I remember, and as I remember, I create.

Her words were meant for you.

You were her companion.

You held her hand and saw the world through her eyes.

There was something in her that always remembered you, felt a longing for your company, like a deep foghorn of a ship sounding in her chest, piercing through the gray, calling for you. She felt your presence and knew you were waiting for her. Then she lost you. Forgot. She almost became normal.

Luna.

Thick, Golden Air

Washington, D.C., USA, July 2007

I swim in the air.
It's thick like water.
I lean forward into it, and it carries me.
The air holds me and moves me.
It is in me and around me, and I swim-fly in it.

I used to do this a lot before we moved to America.

In the forest by the cottage, down by the beach, in Sigrid's garden, in the park, and in the countryside where Grandma lived.

Here in D.C. there are not so many places to swim-fly. This makes me sad.

I used to be able to wander off by myself and find a spot by some trees, or on the beach, or anywhere there was a particularly good feeling, and then I would make myself merge with that, and do my swim-flying.

There isn't much nature around our house here, apart from the trees in our little backyard, and I'm no longer supposed to wander off by myself. This is particularly annoying now during the summer vacation. My friend Geraldine has gone to visit her grandma in New Jersey, and I don't want to do another summer camp without her. We did an art and writing camp together before she left.

I have decided that it is good to use my time writing instead of being bored. It makes me think about things. Often it makes me think about you, Dad. And about Sigrid. I don't know if that is good, but that's what happens when I am stuck here with the babysitters. It doesn't seem right to call the people who watch me babysitters, as I am not a baby, obviously. I would not be writing this if I were a baby. I will soon be a teenager, to be precise. But that's what they call themselves – babysitters. But Mr. Evans is different from the others. He is a schoolteacher. He doesn't want to be called a babysitter. He says it is a term associated with young girls, and that he wants to be called a tutor instead. He comes to my house three times a week. I have to study with him for three hours before we go to the swimming pool.

Adults seem strange to me. I can see what they are thinking and feeling, and I know that most of the time they do or say something completely different than what they really mean. If I point this out, by asking questions, they don't like it, so I have learned not to say anything. I wonder if you are like that too?

I told Mom that I could swim in the air.

She said I must have dreamt it at night, and went on nagging me about my studies and spending more time with other kids, taking up cheerleading or volunteering or something. Anything but being by myself so much. She says being alone takes me away from the real world, and then strange fantasies come.

I still wonder if the people I meet can swim-fly in the air.

You see, through the thick, golden air, I know everything that is going on, behind me, above me, in front of me. I feel like a fish who knows it is living in water. I can see and feel the waves created by other people. Those waves move me. I know who the others are, not their names or what they like for dinner, but the particular feeling there is in the light they have in them. Sometimes I meet someone who also knows they are being moved by the golden air. Then it is possible to swim-fly together. I think that must be what love is.

Some days I wonder if Mom is right, though. About my imagination being too strong, and that I should focus on being in the real world as I grow up. "One day you will need to pay rent and save for retirement!" Mom says. "That day will come sooner than you think!" she says. I'm not sure if she means the rent or the retirement, but Mom says it's very important to save for the retirement, so I have started putting some of my pocket money in a box. Just in case. When I start thinking like that it's not so easy to swim-fly anymore. I get this heavy feeling, like a buffalo is sitting on my head.

I admit that it has become a secret project of mine to look for people who can swim-fly with me. Particularly adults, because maybe, if there are adults who know about this, and who still go to work, and make breakfast, and mow the lawn, and wash their cars, then I will have more proof that Mom is wrong, that she simply is blind to the possibility that swim-flying is as real as what she believes is real, like macaroni and cheese, or the bird poop on the car windshield in the morning.

I wonder if there is a job I can do when I grow up where I can swim-fly in the air. This is what I am trying to figure out, and it's also one of the reasons why I am writing to you, because you know what I am talking about, don't you?

When you read this you will feel the thick, golden air behind my words, and you will know me.

I shall continue writing to you until I find you. Because I need to meet you, and to have a long conversation with you about life and how to be in the real world and also be able to swim-fly in golden light. I would like you to show me that this is possible, before it is too late for me. And I would like you to tell Mom that this thick, golden air is real, and that she is in it too.

It would be really good if you drove a car and had learned to do parallel parking and could also fill in forms and have a job, and still be able to swim-fly. You see, I get the impression from Mom that you couldn't do any of those things when she knew you. She tells me you were a waste of space, a useless wannabe artist and a crazy-maker, and that you avoided driving a car because you were no good at parallel parking.

I wonder if you still live in Greece, on that small island, or have you moved to London? Mom said she thought you might be in London, but then she also said you probably never managed to get your act together and leave.

I have seen a photo of you, and I must say that you looked rather golden, and I wouldn't be surprised if you knew exactly what I am talking about. I am scared that I am a waste of space too, so I am doing my best to figure all of this out before it is too late. And I am trying not to be a crazy-maker, but sometimes Mom calls me just that. Maybe that is what she calls the people she loves. She says she did love you a long time ago, before she found out just how useless you were.

Will you please write me a letter?

It is getting urgent. I will tell you more later. I will include an envelope with my address and a stamp on it and send it to the little island, hoping you are not in London. I don't know what street you live on, but if I write your name on it, I'm sure the postman will find you. Your island must be very tiny. On the photo Mom showed me you stood next to a donkey.

They Lose Their Colors as Soon as They Are Captured

Washington, D.C., USA, August 2007

"We can see them in the night or in the early morning, transformed into adults with wings. Dragonflies have no commercial value compared to butterflies. As soon as they are captured, they lose their colors. That is probably why collectors never pay much attention to them."

I read this in the biology book Mr. Evans made me study last week.

It gives me a queer feeling when I see "adults with wings." I am trying to understand why. Does it make you feel anything? I get a surge through my body, up from my tummy, into my chest and face. Like a whirlwind moving through me. I wonder what that is about. I asked Mr. Evans, but he said that he was not interested in what went on in the lower regions of a prepubescent girl. He said he only cares about what goes on in my brain. I thought that was a very surprising attitude for a teacher, not to be more curious about the strange things happening in the body in response to studying. The brain is obviously part of the body, but I had this feeling he was telling me my brain was separate. Very strange, as I feel I can think with my whole body, not just with my head, and something about those lines from my schoolbook keeps disturbing me.

I am trying to think only with my brain now as I want to do my assignment in a way that makes Mr. Evans happy, but all this swirling in my body is making it hard to focus. I used to think about dragonflies a lot when I was younger, because Grandfather loved the shiny blue ones. He called them *Øyenstikkere.* In Norwegian this means something that stings your eyes. I thought it peculiar that Grandfather would love something so dangerous. But I don't think of them so much anymore. Fireflies are my thing now.

Where I come from there are no fireflies. When I first saw the gardens here in America lit up by those little flying creatures, I thought fairies were dancing all around me. The little lights seemed to be going off completely at random, but as I sat down to observe them, I started to suspect that they were pulsating in a particular rhythm, blinking in response to the same underlying pulse.

I asked Jennifer if she had noticed any patterns in the blinking of fireflies. She had not. Jennifer babysits me sometimes when Mr. Evans is not around. She lives next door and works from home. I can pretty much do what I want when I'm with her, either in her house or in mine. We had lunch together yesterday, and she told me how she used to collect fireflies in a glass jar as a girl, and kept them in her bedroom at night to see the lights flash on and off.

I wonder how long the fireflies can go on shining in a glass jar. I must ask her: how long did it take before the lights became little black stick bodies at the bottom of the glass?

She also told me that she used to think her method of gathering light was superior to her brother's. He and his friends, she said, ripped the wings off the fireflies and smashed them in their hands to see whether their skin would still light up when the flies were dead. But there is no point in collecting dead fireflies. The light fades quickly, and the flies are only interesting when lit up. A brief moment of intense light, that's all.

I am thinking that there would be no point in collecting dead dragonflies either.

Then I think about butterflies and how people collect them and sell them for money. I once went to an exhibition with Uncle Jakob where they sold dried butterflies, and he said that you could get a lot of money from those little creatures, because they keep the color of their wings even through death.

I wonder what happens to the light I see in people's bodies after they die. Have you ever seen a dead person, or been there when someone is dying? Does the light come out of their body, and can it go into someone else's body, like when the boys were crushing the fireflies to get hold of the light?

Gray Strings

Washington, D.C., USA, August 2007

I want to tell you about the time I read a magazine in Sigrid's house. It had lots of interesting things in it, like what authors and painters think about life. We don't have those kinds of magazines in my house, so I was trying to read as much as I could before Sigrid called for me. I was reading about a man who said he was "feeling crushed by the responsibility of being a human being." Do you know what I mean when I say that?

I was standing in the large living room, by the open veranda door. The summer breeze touching my dress gave me goosebumps and sent shivers up my spine. I could hear Sigrid and her father playing on the lawn, chasing Ariel the dog.

They were laughing. Sigrid's mother was in the kitchen and I could hear her talking on the phone. She did not know that I was in the living room. "I can't just leave them now," she said. "I can't do that to Sigrid, she loves her father. You have to be patient! I don't want to have an argument on the phone... of course... I am doing my best, you have to be patient. Yes, I will see you tomorrow night, I love you, it's just that…"

Then I turned a page and saw the headline: "The intense light can be overwhelming. I sometimes feel crushed by the responsibility of being a human being." I have memorized those words. I think it was a poet who said them. I guess they use those special kinds of words. My heart started beating very fast, and I had this loud beeping sound in my right ear. The beep in the ear is what happens when there is something I need to pay attention to in the moment, and it works quite well for that.

Then Sigrid called for me, and her mother walked into the living room. She looked me straight in the eyes, and I looked back at her, and she knew that I knew, and her neck got red as if she had just walked through a shrub of stinging nettles. And I stood there staring at her, wondering what it might be like to love someone who wasn't your husband, and then to cook dinner for your family, and sit down to eat with them and pretend that everything was normal. What she was feeling inside had to be pretty tricky, I thought.

And then I wondered if Mom had done what Sigrid's mom was doing... met someone else. I don't know what happened when you and Mom split up. Was it really just that you did not like each other anymore, or were there other people you had started loving? It's a shame you didn't hang around just a bit longer.

Sigrid and her dad came back from the garden, with Ariel biting the dad's trousers legs, and they saw the mom and me standing there staring at each other like two wild animals. Sigrid froze, and shouted, "Mom, what's the matter?"

She ignored her and said to me, "Put that magazine back where you found it! It's not for children. You need to go home now! We are having dinner, and after that Sigrid will do her homework."

The beeping in my ear was very strong. I looked at Sigrid and her dad. They had golden threads of love between them, and the dog knew this and was swimming and jumping in the thick golden air. And I looked at the mom, felt sorry for her as the golden air was seeping out of her. It seemed like her body was there in the room, but she was not really there, if you know what I mean. Gray strings were pulling at her, making her shatter into many pieces. I would have given her a hug, but instead I left.

My Favorite Tree

Washington, D.C., USA, August 2007

There is a corner in our backyard with a big rock. I love that place. Overhanging branches reach into our yard from the neighbor's side. I'm not sure what the tree is called. It has large thorns, and its branches are twisted and crooked like an old witch's arms and fingers. Its yellow little fruits smell like a mix of oranges and lemons. I sometimes sit on that rock, feeling the tree behind me, smelling those little fruits. I have tried eating them, but they taste bitter and make my mouth go all funny and furry inside. I picked the fruit and took them to my bedroom yesterday. The orangey-lemony smell fills the whole top floor of our house.

Have you ever paid attention to trees? I mean really looked at them? Like whether they are happy or sad?

I like to make myself really quiet inside, and then stand next to a tree. I feel through my body and into the tree. You know, when I do that, the tree notices, and it does exactly the same back to me. Whatever there is in that tree that is alive, comes to meet me. When I do this, which by the way isn't the same as thinking about the tree, I know the kind of life that is moving through it. You can try this for yourself. If you stand still, the trees will find you, and they will know you. Imagine how crazy Mr. Evans would be if I told him that!

When I remember this, it's impossible to feel lonely or lost. I imagine that the trees are my family. The Oak in our backyard is a kind grandfather. I sit with my back against his strong trunk when I feel small. The Ash tree is speedy and brave, a superhero big brother, shooting fiery branches up towards the sky. There is an Ash down in the park that I sometimes visit when I'm feeling scared and don't know what to do. The Azaleas in our front yard may not be trees, but I think of them as my beautiful cousins who come to visit in the spring, all dressed up in amazing red. The Cherry trees along our street are my aunties, and when they bloom, my head spins with happiness, as they are the most beautiful aunties I could ever wish for. I dress up in my finest summer dress and walk up and down our street just to be with them. They tell me stories about their travels to Japan, about visits to palaces and gardens, and having tea with geishas.

I have no idea about the name of the thorny tree. It is kind, wise, old and a bit frightening. It knows things. I think this tree likes me, and when I sit on my rock, I imagine the tree caressing my hair with its ancient hands.

I am sure that plants talk to each other through their fragrances. Their scent becomes their words, only much finer, more like music. Maybe that is why flowers like music. Grandma used to tell me that her tomato plants in the greenhouse were much happier and made sweeter tomatoes when she played classical music on the little radio she kept in there. I remember the smell in that greenhouse: a sharp green, mixed with a round, tangy red geranium scent. I could smell when the tomatoes were ripe, because the sharp green got sweeter and softer and it felt warmer in there. I loved sitting in the glasshouse smelling, listening to music. I used to feel like I was one of the plants in there, absorbing the warm light and being fed by the music.

Mom always says I have a particular fragrance that is uniquely mine. It comes from the area around my neck, by my skull. I like it when she sniffs me there. I feel she knows me then. She says my smell is a kind of peachy, warm, summery smell, and that she would recognize it anywhere. All my clothes smell of this she says. But I cannot smell my own smell. I once asked Uncle Jakob if he thought I had a particular smell. "No, you smell just OK, don't worry," he said. I didn't ask anything else, as he clearly didn't understand.

I think it might be my peachy smell that makes the trees like me. Perhaps that's how I talk to them, and that's how they know who I really am, through my smell. I guess I have more in common with trees and plants than with many people. Plants are particularly interested in light, like me. They stretch towards it, and keep working on their photosynthesis, converting light into energy. "Photo" comes from the Greek language and means light, and "synthesis" means putting together. Putting light together, that's what the trees are doing. This is necessary for having life on earth.

I am studying trees with Mr. Evans, and have to learn the Latin names of many of them. Quercus ilex is Oak, and Fraxinus excelsior is Ash. I like the name Fraxinus for Ash. It really sounds like a superhero.

The Saint

Washington, D.C., USA, September 2007

It's the first week back at school after the summer vacation, and I'm in trouble.

I'm in trouble with Mom, and also with Mr. Finnley, my science teacher.

Mom said I have been a crazy-maker again, so I am grounded for two weeks. I have to reflect on what I did so that I can understand that actions have consequences. And I have to be serious about my homework so I can improve. Also, I can say goodbye to my pocket money for two weeks.

I promise to do my homework as soon as I have finished writing to you. I need to tell you a couple of things first, because you probably are the only one who would understand. I know that I don't know you really, I'm aware of that, of course, because I am not really crazy or anything like that, I know that I'm not. It's a different thing altogether being a crazy-maker than being crazy. When you are a crazy-maker, you make other people crazy, people like Mom, and I understand that it's not a good thing for other people to be crazy because of me. I don't like Mom to be crazy. So I know that I don't know you yet, but I know that I will, as soon as you read this, you will write back to me, and we will know each other.

Anyway, today's trouble has been about a major incident to do with light. It has raised many new questions for me in terms of what this light is. I will try to describe it as accurately as possible. I am worried that I will not be able to put it into words that will fit if I wait a long time before I write to you, so even though I promised Mom not to think about light for a long time, here I am writing to you. The light is still in me, so you might be able to feel it through my words if you make yourself really quiet inside.

I did not go to school today, which caused Mr. Finnley to call Mom. He has been asked to contact her if I don't show up. Not that I often miss school, don't get me wrong! I do like learning. It's just that sometimes special things happens, and I have to check them out. Well, this happened today and caused Mom to leave an important meeting at work, which made her very angry. I am a bit ashamed to say that the police were contacted as well, because no one knew where I was, and my phone was switched off. In this country they think there are bad people lurking everywhere, and that kids need constant surveillance. There is just no freedom, which sometimes drives me crazy. Anyway, the reason why I didn't go to school today is that a saint from India is staying in the hotel at the end of our street this week. Now, I'm sure you understand that this is an exceptional event. But that's why I'm writing to you, and not to Mom or to Mr. Finnley. I do feel bad for Mom, but then again…

Here's what happened. On my way to school I walked past the hotel. Normally there isn't much going on there, just taxis coming and going, and people looking confused, walking around in circles, or looking like actors on a film set, all dressed up, moving in straight lines to very important meetings. I have sometimes gone into the lobby just to sense what it might be like to be those people. The funny thing is, it's as if I became invisible when I walk into the lobby, because neither the disorientated people, nor the sharp ones ever see me. I feel scared of the straight-lined people, because they move quickly and I really don't think they see anyone who is smaller, or slower than themselves. And the other kind doesn't see me either, because they are so preoccupied with trying to figure out where they are and what is going on. Anyway, this morning was different. There was a crowd outside the hotel, with many people wearing white, and looking as if they were from India. And they moved differently. And when I stopped to look at them, some even noticed me. One woman smiled and said, "We'd better get in line. It's going to be a long day. Long and beautiful!" And then she walked off and disappeared into the lobby. I heard the sharp, loud beep in my ear and forgot all about school. I followed the beep and the smiling lady into the hotel.

There were large posters of an Indian-looking lady hanging all over the lobby. I asked a man where everyone was going, and he said that they were heading to the large conference hall to meet the Saint. The word Saint came tripping off his tongue as if he had said rice-pudding, or something normal like that, but I am certain he said Saint. My head went empty. In my life no one ever talks about saints, other than when not wanting to do something for someone else, like: "Do you think I'm some kind of saint ?!?" But this was different. The beep was loud, so I followed the man's pointing finger.

I walked right into a line of people waiting in front of closed double doors. There was a woman there, and everyone was looking at her. She was dressed in white, with an orange scarf around her neck. I turned to the man behind me and asked if the woman with the orange scarf was the Saint. He grinned behind his large beard, saying that she might be a saint, but not the one he had come to meet. The Saint, he said, was behind the doors, getting ready. He asked me if I had a ticket. I shook my head, thinking it sounded strange that I needed a ticket to see a saint.

I suddenly remembered waiting in line at the fairground with Uncle Jakob when he came to visit a few years ago. We had gone there for the main attraction of that summer, the new water and air ride. Uncle Jakob had left me standing in line while he went to purchase tickets in a little booth nearby. I remember the feeling I had in my tummy as I was waiting, like a yummy but painful pressure of being so near something incredible... like someone was promising me ice cream and a puppy dog, and a holiday with *you*, my mysterious father, all at once... I mean that's what I thought of as joy back then, and even Uncle Jakob had promised to ride with me on this new rollercoaster of pure joy. I wished that Uncle Jakob were here with me now, getting tickets to see the Saint together. Although I don't really believe Uncle Jakob would have been very interested in spending the morning lining up to see a saint. It wouldn't be his idea of an interesting event.

I think *you* probably would have done that… Is that right?

Dad?

Would you have done that?

Would the beep in the ear that makes the world stop, the calling from the soft spot inside, have kept you in line to see something you didn't understand? Like when you suddenly see something strange in the middle of what you think ordinary, and which you have stopped seeing, because it's so ordinary, and when that soft spot starts going wild you forget about yourself and your little life, like whether Mr. Finnley will like your homework, or if Sally will invite you to her birthday party, or leave you out like she did last year. Or if your mom will be OK, or if you will ever meet someone you are longing for?

All of this went through my head as I stood in line in that stuffy hotel, waiting to see the Saint. And then a man handed out tickets, and I stopped thinking because I had to focus on what was happening. He gave me a green piece of paper with the letter C on it. I asked how much it was to see the Saint. He laughed and said that I had already paid, and now it was time to receive. I was very confused, but it sounded good to me. Although the thought of money was also bad, because I knew I would have to say goodbye to my pocket money when Mom learned about this. I wanted to phone her to explain, tell her about this situation. Like, if I told her I was engaged in a learning experience, an educational field trip, then maybe she would say that this was good and I'd better stay here than going to school. She is always going on about how important it is to be curious about other cultures. She sometimes travels herself to faraway places on her way to stop poverty in the world. She is very good with numbers. She cannot travel much anymore, though, so she might like me telling her about all those people from India down the road. Thinking about it this way, I almost felt certain that she would like what I was doing. But then I remembered her saying that discipline and integrity are the two main ingredients of success, and in getting anywhere worthwhile in the world. And if I did not build those muscles of discipline and integrity now, I would end up like you, who had not built this into your system at an early age, and got sidetracked by fools' gold and cheap promises of miracles at every corner. That's what she says. I asked her what fools' gold was, and if she thought you had seen any miracles, and that I was really interested in finding out whether miracles could happen, and then she got annoyed and told me that those were figures of speech, meaning that you avoided responsibility and reality at all costs. Remembering this made me less sure of how I would explain where I was to Mom.

Then the doors opened and I forgot everything about Mom. From my place in the line I could see parts of the hall. On one side there was a stage decorated with flowers and surrounded by colorful drapes on the walls. In the middle of the stage was a small orange platform covered with white silk and orange and purple cushions. There were three Indian-looking men and one woman wearing white and orange, standing behind that little platform.

As we moved into the hall I could hear music playing. A woman was singing and her voice made me feel like I was swimming in the air. I followed the person in front of me who sat down on a chair three rows from the stage. Then one of the men on the stage spoke into a microphone. I couldn't understand what he was saying, though, because of his thick accent. There was a smell in the air, like a sweet flowery burning kind of smell. I turned around and saw that all the chairs behind me were filled, and people were still coming into the room. Then another man spoke in the microphone, and now I could hear words like,

"Before she enters… field of stillness, quieting our minds…

breathing together… receive her gifts." I didn't know what this meant, but he started singing "Ooooooom," and everyone joined in with him, so I did as well. Although it felt odd to sit there singing "Ooooooom" with a lot of strangers, it was also kind of familiar, almost as if this were something Mom and I did after dinner every day. The thought of this made me giggle. After a while everyone stopped singing and the man said in the microphone, "Now rest in the stillness that creates everything." People were closing their eyes, so I did too, and I must tell you, it was a bit like jumping into a dark pool of water. I could see colors dancing all around, purple and gold, and the dark was alive, and moved in my body and outside of me. This dark was a golden dark. Very strange, because it was like luminous darkness, like the darkness was light. Do you know what I mean?

And then she was there. A small woman. Not thin, that's not what I mean when I say small. She was just not very tall, but kind of fleshy. Her body looked so soft, the softest body I have ever seen, like water or soft clay. There was a lot of her, but at the same time she looked almost transparent, like the molecules of her body were not densely glued together, but I could see them dancing and spinning around in light. Looking at her made me think of how Mr. Finnley talks about the electrons spinning around the nucleus of an atom. He says the electrons are attracted to the nucleus. I wondered why I saw this when looking at the woman up there. It's not as though I had actually seen the electrons dancing around the center of the atom. But I could kind of see that happening in her. In class I imagined the negatively charged electrons being in love with the positively charged center, spinning around looking for an opening to join with the power in the nucleus, and I thought it was that love that the electrons felt that kept the whole thing together and moving forever. (Don't worry, I will never actually write this in a paper for Mr. Finnley; it's only to you that I say these things.) And then it felt like all the people in the room, all of us, had become electrons orbiting around the nucleus of power that was her. She seemed to be attracting us by electricity or magnetism, or love... and, actually, I think we all longed to collapse into her, in the same way that I imagine electrons longing to collapse into the center of the atom.

Then I looked at the Saint and I wanted to cry and laugh at the same time. I don't think I have ever felt like this before. The beeping in my ear went crazy.

People in the front row left their seats and went up to the platform, and believe it or not, the Saint started hugging them. Each one went down on their knees in front of her, and she took them in her arms as if they were her long-lost babies, held them for a while, and whispered something in their ears. I was really shocked to see grown-ups throw themselves into her arms. Mom would never do that! Neither would Uncle Jakob or Mr. Finnley. I don't think I know any adult who would do that.

Some people came out of the hug with tears streaming down their faces, others smiling, and others again with faces that looked calm and relaxed, as if she had taken all their troubles away. Now I was really intrigued about this woman, but then the person to my right nudged me, and it was time for me to go up and be hugged. My tummy tightened, and I had a moment of doubt, thinking that I had gotten lost into a place where I did not belong, and that I should focus on the real physics in my textbook rather than this kind of experiment, but I was already being pushed up towards the platform. A woman asked me to remove my shoes and to leave my schoolbag by the side of the stage. I climbed the five steps to the platform where another woman took my arm and placed me facing the Saint. I was pushed down, my head in her lap. I didn't have time to think whether this was a good place or not. I disappeared into a soft sea, and in a sweet smell of flowers, and all my crazy thoughts disappeared. She held me tight, but it was soft. I felt like a sugar lump melting into her dark, warm, luminous body. I heard her repeating in my ear, "You are my daughter, you are my daughter, you are my daughter." She kissed my forehead, and I was grabbed by someone who nudged me to the left side and down some steps, and I felt my legs sway, so I sat down on the carpeted floor, feeling like I had been spun around, shot out to outer space and sunk into the deepest sea at the same time. I felt completely still, and like not needing anything, because everything was already in me and around me. I have never felt this before, not needing anything, not wanting anything to be different, even slightly, not even worrying about Mom, but feeling totally alive in a way that wasn't how I normally think of me feeling alive and happy. It was as if there was no time. And it was silent.

I thought I had only sat there for a moment when someone tapped me on the shoulder. It was the man with the beard who had stood behind me in the line. He sat down next to me and asked if I was hungry. "Not really," I said, "I just had breakfast."

"I don't think so." He smiled, and said that it was almost 6pm, and that he had watched me sit there all day. "It's called bliss," he said. "It can make you forget about food. Now come with me and have something to eat."

So he took me to a side room where they sold curries and cakes, and he bought me a curry and we sat down at a table. He asked if it was my first time to see her, and I said it was. "It can be a strong experience to be embraced by the Shakti," he said. I was not sure what he meant with "Shakti"; I thought maybe it was the Saint's name.

Then I walked up the road and saw that all the lights were on in our house. Mom was on the phone, pacing around in the living room. I opened the door, still feeling the light in my body. Mom's shrill voice became a wild wave crashing against my chest. Her hand raised up above her head. Came down on my face. Still calm inside. How edgy her movements were. A hand raised up again. Came down on my shoulder. My knees swayed.

Sank down on the floor. Sat there for a long time. Under water. Heard her voice. Called the police. Said, "She is home."

I'm in my room now and it is cold. I don't like the rainy fall here, it's damp and miserable and everything feels soggy. I sit in my bed with my physics book in front of me. I open the book and see black signs on a paper, like little dead insects. I can't make any sense of them. I wish I could hug Mom. I hear the television downstairs. Mom is watching BBC World News by herself in the living room. She will be angry with me for many days, and probably not talk to me for a while. This is because I am a crazy-maker and I upset Mom. This is bad for her. Really bad. And now I should probably tell you why.

(I wish I had your phone number. It would be nice to hear your voice now. It is good to write to you, but if I could call you, I would know that you are really listening.)

Dead Fish Eyes

Washington, D.C., USA, September 2007

I cannot make her crazy because I want to make her better.

She's been to the hospital again.

If you loved her a long time ago, perhaps there is still a little spot in your heart that feels warmth for her. Now would be a good time to pull out that warmth and send it her way.

I find it very difficult to look at her face when she comes back from the hospital. She is all white, and her eyes are like the eyes of the fish on ice in the supermarket. There is a bit more life in her than in the dead fish, of course, but the emptiness is there. I used to go look at the eyes of those fishes, just to have a feeling of what the difference was between being alive and moving, like I was, and being dead, like them. I would stare into the black eyes, and this used to make me want to run and jump, just to make sure that I was really alive. I was a bit younger then. I have stopped doing that now. Instead, I now look into the eyes of the people who work in the shop, because sometimes they have dead-fish eyes too, as if they had become things, like the things that they beep the food with, and the customers don't see that they are human beings any more, and treat them like machines. I want to bring back some light in those eyes, but I don't know how to do it, and it upsets me. I'm scared of becoming a thing. And that's how Mom's eyes are when she has been to the hospital. I think that the machines that are meant to make her better are making her eyes look dead instead, and she becomes a bit like a thing, and I have to spend a long time reminding her that she is a human being. I put on her favorite music, I tell her that I love her, and remind her of the colors of the flowers in the garden and the different shapes of the leaves on all the trees out there. Then slowly her eyes get a bit of light in them, and I have noticed that if I manage to come up with something special, like writing a little poem, or describing a flower particularly well, or reminding her of how Grandpa used to look after all the animals that she loved on the farm where she grew up, then sometimes there is a flash in her heart. I can feel it in my chest just as it happens in her heart, like we are completely linked or something. When I feel this flash in her, and look into her eyes, it seems that the lights have been switched on again, and she is not a thing anymore, but a human being, until next time she goes to the hospital and the babysitter comes to stay with me.

I wish you could stay with me instead!

Uncle Jakob

Washington, D.C., USA, October 2007

Do you remember Uncle Jakob? I tried to call him today. I wanted to ask him if he had found a new girlfriend yet. He changes girlfriends quite often, and I heard that he was not with Mia anymore. He didn't pick up my call so I left a message.

Uncle Jakob lives in a large white apartment with a lot of windows and tall ceilings. That's common in Norway. I only saw Mia on the computer as we Skyped one Sunday. She was in the background and came to say hello. She was pretty in a non-complicated way, if you know what I mean. Her face and her body and her hair were all in agreement with one another. I noticed this because it's unlike what I see in most people, who seem to have a constant argument going on between their hair and their body and their brain and their hearts, and where some days the hair wins, and it becomes what they call a good hair day, but a bad body day, but at least it's a good hair day, so then the hair is making all the decisions that day. Anyway, I wondered what it might be like, spending the summer with Mia, what it might feel like to be sitting next to her... if my body and hair and brain and heart would become smoothed out and less complicated in her presence. All of this I thought in the short moment that she came to say hello, holding a glass of orange juice, stroking Uncle Jakob's back, tilting her head to the right and smiling so that we would like her. I did like her. And I knew that Mom had been talking to Uncle Jakob about me going to stay with him in the summer, as she didn't want a repeat of this year's vacation, which she thought had been bad for me. And also, if I went to stay with Uncle Jakob, she wouldn't have to worry about me while she went to the hospital, because Mia, who is a university teacher, would have time to spend with me.

I have to tell you that I felt very excited about the thought of going to Norway for the whole summer, to be with Mia, and to see Sigrid again. But I also felt worried for what might happen to Mom if I was not there to make her human after her visits to the hospital. And I know that she would be spending too much time in the office, in front of the computer, talking to people on the phone about numbers and projects and money and poor women in Africa, and never really taking time to go out in the garden, or to look at the fireflies or the stars at night, but just worrying about those poor women in Africa, and by the time I would come back from Norway she would have turned into a thing, trying to save the lives of those poor, poor women, but there would be no life in her eyes, and I didn't think it was worth me going to see Uncle Jakob and Mia and Sigrid if that would happen. Maybe Mom would be better off having a crazy-maker around. Being a crazy-maker, reminding her of you and your search for miracles, might not be so bad after all.

I really think it would be so sad if everything in the world became like everything else, if you know what I mean by that.

But Uncle Jakob told Mom that Mia was no longer his girlfriend. She had annoyed him too much, made him feel like "a bad egg." From the top of the stairs, I listened to Mom Skyping with him in Norwegian, which I love listening to. I wanted to understand everything they said, in case they discussed things about me, where I would go if Mom was in hospital, or even if Mom told Uncle Jakob things about her sickness that she was hiding from me. I wrote down the Norwegian words which I didn't know, and Googled them afterwards to see what they meant in English. Some I couldn't find as they were probably not at all spelt the way I wrote them down. However, after I looked things up, I learned the meaning of narcissistic, pathetic, intellectual, misogynist, misanthrope, and adoring female.

Jakob said he was loving staying up all night, drinking whisky and reading *My Struggle*, a book that Mia thought was "narcissistic and pathetic," while Uncle Jakob thought it was "an intellectual masterpiece." Apparently, he was now enjoying "having the freedom to be a narcissist and a misanthrope, without a squeaky-clean Miss Apple Pie making me feel bad about it." He also said that next time he would choose a woman who was not such a "perfect product of the healthy, conformist lie of expensive Goretex rain jackets and PhDs." Next time he would go for a "Mediterranean, hot-blooded woman who didn't have to show the world how smart she was." I'm not sure what this all meant, even after looking up the meaning of the words.

"You're a misogynist," replied Mom. "You got that from Dad. And you're cynical! There is no way that I will send my daughter to stay with you. I thought Mia would have a healthy effect on you, but you are beyond hope. Enjoy your sour, male literature and your whisky while waiting for the perfect, non-existing, ever-adoring female. You are like most men."

The conversation made me feel very heavy, and I had a kind of sticky sensation in my tummy. I noticed that the space seemed to close down around me as I heard them talking, and it was hard to breathe.

Mom told Uncle Jakob that she at least hoped she could count on him to come over if she had to stay in hospital for a longer period. I heard her ask if he had signed the papers for taking me if she should go. Uncle Jakob answered that he didn't have much choice but to sign, as there was no one else, and if he didn't sign, the Americans would put me in a children's home and view me as their property. I found this very strange, that I could be viewed as the property of America.

How can a person be someone's property?

Mom also told Uncle Jakob that Jennifer and Katherine, our neighbors on the left side, had also signed the papers for taking care of me in emergency situations, until he could fly over and get me.

This conversation taught me some new things. I read on the

Internet that misogynist means "one who hates or mistrusts women," and I found it strange. My impression was that Uncle Jakob loved too many women. Anyhow, the point is that they had dropped the idea of me going to stay with him in the summer. This was a relief, as I could focus on keeping Mom well. But also a disappointment as I really wanted to see Sigrid, and to go to all my favorite spots by the sea.

I wouldn't have had to listen to all of this if you were around. Even if you weren't living with us, if you were somewhere not too far away, I wouldn't have had to hear all of that.

I wonder if Mom will ever love a man again.

Mom says you met Uncle Jakob many times, and that you sort of liked each other, but that you were very different. I think Mom said once that since Grandpa did not like you, Uncle Jakob automatically liked you, and that whenever there was a family occasion, he would loudly tell everyone how fantastic it was that you and Mom were together. It was not very often that the whole family got together, mostly Christmas, and some summer times, Mom told me.

If you have ever been to the area where Uncle Jakob lives – even though he always complains about where he lives, he has never moved – then you might have gone down to my favorite beach. I hope you did. If you did, then you understand why I so would like to visit Uncle Jakob again. You moved to an island, so you understand. You probably love the ocean as much as I do. Maybe it was from you I got this. Do you think this kind of love can be passed on through the genes? I should ask Mr. Finnley about that. He likes talking about genes in class.

Sigrid

Washington, D.C., USA, October 2007

Uncle Jakob's apartment is near Sigrid's house. She still lives there, with both her parents. The dog Ariel is dead.

Sigrid and I Skype each other, but it's not so easy. Sometimes I think that it's easier to have a relationship with someone you are writing to than with someone you only see on a screen. We tell each other what has happened at school, and Sigrid tells me about the fun new friends she has, and what they all do together at the weekends. In the summer, they meet up down by the beach and "hang out." There are some older boys and Sigrid really likes one called Oscar. She giggles when she talks about him, and says he grabbed her and tried to throw her in the water, and that it was crazy, but I can see that she really liked it, and that she feels special because Oscar did that. She emailed a photo of him, and he looked like an advert kind of boy, like the ones you see with long hair and bronzed skin, wearing expensive trainers. He was very handsome. I didn't know what I should send her in return as I don't have any photos of boys. I don't think she would be interested seeing the tree in my back yard.

Sigrid's mom didn't leave them. We never spoke about what I heard that day. It's strange because I felt that I used to know Sigrid from the inside, but now it's like she only wants to know me from the outside, and I feel I must have exciting stories to tell her. Mostly I don't know what to say to her anymore. Once I tried to tell her that Mom is sick and goes to the hospital and comes back home with dead eyes, but she said she had to rush out to catch a ride to soccer training, and that was it.

I figured it was better not tell her about the Saint.

The last time we spoke I wanted to ask her if she ever went down to the beach by herself, like we used to do when I lived there. I often went down there early in the morning, when the sun was coming up, just to sit by the water. Sometimes I would find Sigrid on the beach. Those mornings used to fill me up with a kind of smooth honey feeling that would last for the whole day. Everything would become completely shiny and clear, empty and full and beautiful, and all the things I looked at were gleaming, light shining, and I would swim-fly in this sea of thick, transparent air that breathed everything and moved everything. I remember I asked Sigrid if she felt any of this, and she did. That was back then. I would feel foolish to ask her if she remembered this now. I think I'm probably more childish than she is, at least that's what Mom would say.

But I did think of asking her again the last time we spoke.

The Neighbor

Washington, D.C., USA, October 2007

I am sitting by my desk, and should be concentrating on my homework, not writing to you.

I am working on a piece for my English class, which is due on Friday. We have been reading a bunch of poems, and are supposed to pick one we like and write about it. I chose *The Arrow and The Song* by Henry Wadsworth Longfellow:

I shot an arrow into the air,
It fell to earth, I knew not where;
For, so swiftly it flew, the sight
Could not follow it in its flight.

I breathed a song into the air,
It fell to earth, I knew not where;
For who has sight so keen and strong,
That it can follow the flight of song?

Long, long afterward, in an oak
I found the arrow, still unbroke;
And the song, from beginning to end,
I found again in the heart of a friend.

But now I am looking out of the window. I have been doing this all week. By 4.30pm on the dot, the neighbor comes out into his backyard, and I get caught up in watching him. He walks very, very slowly, tracing a rectangle with his steps. He follows one side of the fence, then turns equally slowly to snail-walk along the short side of the fence. I haven't been able to sit still and watch the whole sequence from beginning to end yet, as it is so slow and I get tired, or I suddenly feel that I need to go to the bathroom, or I want to get a drink or a cookie. It's strange how hard it is to sit still and do nothing other than watch someone move very slowly. Have you ever tried this? I recommend that you do, because you learn a lot about what happens in your head and your body when you try to sit still. I've discovered that a lot of crazy things pass through my head. I don't mean sitting still like I do when watching TV. That is a very different thing, as I forget altogether that I have a body, or my own thoughts, or that I am there at all, as I watch whatever is on TV. That's not what I mean by sitting still and watching something. I'm talking about the way that I can sit still and watch, while also knowing that I am there. I used to be able to sit still and watch the sea and know that I was there. That was not so difficult, as I could hear the sound of the sea and the birds, and I could feel the wind that swept over my face, and I could shiver in the coolness of the morning, or melt a bit in the warmth of the sun, and then just rest in the thick golden air that would appear. Watching the neighbor is a little different. It's more like hard work. Sometimes I experiment by concentrating on the garden, on the trees, and not on the neighbor walking, just to have some variation, but after a little while of watching the trees, it's as if I stopped seeing them, and I only see the thoughts that are going on in my head; like I am not really there, but in a foggy place where thoughts just keep charging through my mind, and I can almost see the thoughts as if they are being printed onto the trees that I am trying to watch. I see Mom lying in the bed. I see Mom in hospital. I see Mom not moving.

I never before realized that it's so hard to see what is there, and not just all the things that are in my head painted on top of what I am trying to see. I am scared that I have forgotten how to look at the sea. I need to get to the sea and check this out. What if my thought-fog would hang over the sea as well, and what if the thick, golden air did not appear anymore?

You see, this is why I really, really wanted to stay with Uncle Jakob this summer. To find out. Do you think it becomes harder to see as we grow up? If it does, I'm a bit scared of growing older. I wonder if it is like that with everything we look at. If it is, then how do we know what anything really is, or how anything came to be, and what anything really means? Like, when I look at the words in the poem from my homework, I start to see so many stories... I could write a whole book about it, and I even see the song from the poem landing in your heart sometimes, and then finding it when I find you. But I'm not sure it will have much to do with what the words of the poem are really saying. How do we ever know anything for what it really is?

Have you noticed how hard it is to really see something? Or do you still see clearly, even if you are an adult? I wonder what Mom sees when she looks at me. I wonder if she ever sees me, just as I am. Do I ever see Mom, as she really is? I'm scared that I don't remember what she looked like before she got sick. I don't want to see sickness when I look at Mom.

Will I be able to see you when I meet you? Or will I just see all the Dad-stories that I have made up about you? For a long time I imagined you like the dad in *Mio, My Son,* a book that Mom read for me when I was little. Mio had to live with his horrible aunt and uncle because his mom was dead, and nobody knew where his dad was. And he longed to meet his dad so much, so much that he almost got crazy, so much did he long for him... almost like those electrons I told you about longing to meet the center of the atom. So much, that one day he entered a magical path to Faraway Land where his dad lived, and it seemed to me that it was the longing in his heart that made that path appear out of nowhere. And the dad was the King of Faraway Land, and the dad had also been searching for Mio, ever since he had been taken away from him shortly after he had been born. I found this part of the story particularly comforting, that what he had been looking for had also been looking for him.

Mio's dad was kind and king-like, and Mio rode around on a white, flying horse in the King's rose gardens and felt that he truly belonged. I wanted to find the path to Faraway Land, and I wanted you to be just like Mio's dad. But I don't think like that anymore. I am trying to think of you more like a normal person now.

These are the kinds of things that go on in my head as I sit and watch the neighbor. Then the strange thing is, that after all this thinking, when I kind of wake up and realize that I have been thinking, and not seen anything at all for ages and ages, and when I look at the neighbor again, then I see that he has hardly moved at all. Like he is moving and not moving at the same time. Like he is doing something to time. Like making it pass and not pass. I get itchy. Go to the bathroom for a break, eat a cookie, and as I turn back to him, he is there, gliding slowly on the grass without ever fidgeting or doing any sudden movements. He seems to get clearer and clearer as he walks, as if the thought-fog that I could see over the trees were being blown away. When I watch him, my body also gets more slow and still, and my head more quiet. It's a bit like looking through a camera, and at first the lens is out of focus and the outlines are fuzzy, but as he moves slowly, the lens gets focused, and I start to see very clearly the outlines of his body. The colors all around him get brighter and more sparkly. When he turns to walk up the second long side of the rectangle, it looks like his shape stands out from the surroundings, and he is shimmering with golden light, as if the snail-walking is filling him up with light. It is as if he is both completely a part of the garden and the trees around him, and also completely standing out from the rest, so I can see him clearly.

By now you probably understand why I feel I have to watch him walk in the garden. Who would have thought that by walking slowly like that, someone can make light appear?

If I manage to sit still and watch him until he completes the rectangle, the thoughts in my head are quiet, and I can see with my whole body again, and everything looks slightly different. Everything is clear and transparent. And I don't have images of Mom being in a hospital bed in my head, and I'm not scared. When I look at the neighbor in this way, I know him.

I have never spoken to him. Mom says he is a weird recluse, a Vietnam veteran who has lost the plot, but who probably is harmless. Mom says that Jennifer told her that he doesn't talk to anyone. His house looks shabby and he never prunes the wild brambles growing along the fence. I guess he prefers spending his time walking slowly rather than pruning the brambles. Once a branch from a huge Oak in his yard fell down on our side during a storm, and Mom wanted to go and talk to him because she felt it was dangerous, and that in the next storm a branch or a whole tree might fall on our house, or on our car, and cause serious damage. She says it is good to have the trees in one's yard seen to by professionals. The Oaks in our yard are pruned and checked once a year, and Jennifer and Katherine on the other side are also very decent when it comes to neighborly duties, Mom says.

But I am thinking that it will not be an Oak that kills Mom.

Mom never went to talk to the neighbor. When I asked why, she said that he probably would not have opened the door anyway, not have taken any heed of her because he was antisocial, and that she didn't feel safe knocking on his door by herself. You don't know what people like that might do if you get on their wrong side, she said. "In this country everyone has a gun... you even bring notices back from school, advising us to keep our guns locked away safely... Back home they gave us warnings about head lice. Here they ask us to look out for guns..."

Then I said that I didn't know anyone who had a gun, and that I had never seen a real gun, and that I could come with her to talk to him, as I was curious to see who he was. This was before I started watching him walk slowly. I haven't told Mom about the snail-walking, as I feel I need to gather some more information about what this really is about.

After the snail-walking, the neighbor usually leaves. This is around 6.30pm. He doesn't have a car, so he walks everywhere, but not slowly like in the garden. His pace is quite fast when he walks on the street. I have once seen him on a bicycle, and I have also seen him waiting at the bus stop once when we were coming back from watching *The Lord of the Rings* on a Friday night. When he goes out in the evenings he wears a big black hat with a floppy brim, black trousers and a dark blue windbreaker jacket. He pulls a black rolling suitcase behind him. He has a big white beard, and I would not say that he looks like most other people around here. This, I don't think is a bad thing, but I guess one could, like Mom does, decide that it all adds up to him being a suspicious kind of person, one that does suspicious kinds of things. I mean, I could have this kind of story in my head while meeting him, and then not see who he is at all. Like think he is some sort of Gollum, and not the shiny person I know from watching him snail-walk.

I wish the neighbor were the poem I am studying for my homework. From watching him snail-walk, and then go out at 6:30pm three evenings a week, I would write about the regularity of his movements, like how Miss Green, my English teacher, talks about the regularity of the rhyme in certain poems. That the beginning of his poem is slow and without rhyme, but with a style that has you think about everything in a new way, a way that is very difficult to understand with your head, and then that the second part of his poem speeds up and becomes more like a rhyming one, which you can make sense of in an ordinary way. Then I would start imagining where he would be going, and what he would be doing there, which probably would have nothing to do with what that poem was really showing. I am trying to imagine what things the neighbor will be doing when he leaves at 6:30pm. Mom says she does not want to imagine anything about where he is going or what he is doing. She wants as much as possible to avoid thinking about the man, the one who is a threat to us by not taking care of his Oaks, she says, and she wants to leave it at that. I find that strange. I cannot just leave it at that. I keep thinking about it. I wish I could be thinking about the poem for my homework instead, because then I would know exactly what to write, and Miss Green would be happy. But I cannot switch off those thoughts. I am hoping that by writing all this down for you, I can sort things out in my head, and go back to my homework again.

My window faces the neighbor's yard and sometimes when I go to the bathroom in the middle of the night I look over at his house, and I see the lights on in his attic. Once I went down into our yard and I stood very quietly under my Oak for what seemed to be a long time, probably 40 minutes or something, and I looked at those lights and listened for clues. There were sounds coming from the attic. Voices. It didn't sound like the TV, with all the advertisings and music breaks. It sounded like real people talking, although I have never seen anyone enter or leave his house. *What if he keeps people captured up there?* I thought. And when this thought bombed my head, I ran back inside and scurried deep into my bed, under the covers, like I used to do when I was five and I was scared of the shadows on my wall, and I used to close my eyes and imagine that you would come and hold me until the scary feelings had gone away.

If there are people up there who need help, and I know that they are there, but I do nothing... then it is really bad. And it gives me the creeps just to think about it. I wish I were brave. How does one become brave? If you were here, I could have told you, and you would have known what to do. I am telling you now, and it's helping a little, but not as much as if you were here. And we could have gone together to knock on his door to see him, talk to him, and get a feeling for what was real. And if we still thought he was a suspicious kind of person after trying to really see him, we could have figured out a plan for how to rescue the people trapped in the attic. I think it would be easier to be brave if you were here. I don't feel very brave as I am writing to you now, not brave at all… I am wondering who is up there... Babies, mothers, animals, dead people, young girls, gypsies, nurses, cheerleaders, old grandmothers, crocodiles, dead people and children, young girls, cats and hamsters, fish, babysitters, teachers, lizards and shop assistants, feet and hands, blond hair in braids, brains and hearts that he brings home in his trolley suitcase. The body of the little man I saw in the wheelchair the other day. The bus driver who always smiles at me in the morning. The rabbit that Geraldine lost in the spring. Butterflies pinned to the walls. The boy who was mean to me down by the creek.

Anyway, that's what comes into my head if I'm not careful. I haven't told Mom, as you know, she would call me a crazy-maker.

The Greatest

Washington, D.C., USA, November 2007

I just wanted to tell you that sometimes I have great times with Mom. Like last Saturday when she took me to the indoor ice-skating rink. We rented white skates, and she showed me how to do spins. Mom could do incredible spirals on the ice. She circled around me. Around and around and around. Then she pulled me into her and we glided around the rink together, and we laughed, and they were playing really loud music, and one of my favorite songs came on, about time moving on and being your number one, and not giving up just like that... And the music and the gliding got into me, and I wanted to skate around and around with Mom forever.

Do they ever play that song on the island where you live?

And then I fell and my trousers got icy and wet, but it was OK, because we had hot chocolate in my favorite cafe. I am sure you know this about Mom, that she can be the greatest, particularly when she is feeling well. Because you loved her.

Just in case my letters made you think that she was not like that anymore. She sometimes is.

The Red Tulip of Hope

Washington, D.C., USA, November 2007

Tonight I'm working on a new project for my English class.

Do you remember the other homework I told you about? The poem? Miss Green liked what I wrote, said that I have a unique way of understanding, and that I am getting better at communicating it. It made me very happy that she said those things. When she looks at me, it feels like what is invisible about me, even to me, becomes visible. It's a kind of inside-out-seeing that she does, and I think she has a special talent for that, which makes me want to go to her class and to study. When I'm with her, my insides start to line up, because she has her insides lined up. It's strange. I have noticed that I can be coming from another class, and feel confused or messy inside, and as soon as I step into Miss Green's room, all of that soupy messiness clears up. She stands there waiting for us all to sit down, and she doesn't do anything that you can see, but she looks at everyone, and the air gets clearer, and she is just there, filling the room with a kind of clarity and a light that shines out of her body, and I can feel that she is all lined up on the inside, so the outside world becomes lined up and clear around her as well. It's easy to think in her classes, and it's fun. I think I love her.

Anyway, she gave us a new writing assignment this week. She wants us to use all our senses to take in the impressions of the night. What we can hear, smell, see, sense, and taste outside when it's dark. She says that impressions are food for us, and they feed our imagination and our energy, and that when it is dark our senses get sharper. She wants us to sit down with our notebooks in a garden or on a doorstep or on a flight of stairs, close our eyes for a moment, and without thinking about it, write down as fast as we can whatever comes to us in response to our senses in the dark. We have to do this for five minutes without stopping.

I wish you could be doing that on your Greek island, and then we could compare our writings.

Anyhow, this is what I wrote:

I am a boat in the dark sea, following the red tulip of hope. The shadow of a cat is a Halloween monster, and the neighbor flies on a borrowed broomstick, landing in the old Oak tree. The smell of damp leaves makes me feel at home. My heart is in the tree, and my head is branching out into the garden of songs.

The Blind Man Who Could See Light

Washington, D.C., USA, November 2007

Something incredible happened yesterday.

Now it is the morning; 7am. I had to write to you as soon as I woke up. Mom is still sleeping. There is light outside, but the night has only just gone. I woke up in twilight, and I had the most incredible feeling in my body. Maybe you have had this, too, this feeling that something really good has happened, but you cannot quite remember what it was, as the sleep is still in your brain, so there is just this wordless feeling of wonder in your body.

I made myself lie very still, as if not to scare that feeling away.

As I was being still and my bedroom got flooded with dawn, the reason for the feeling landed on me. Yesterday morning Mom emptied her bag on the dining table to find her keys, took out a book that I had not seen before, and put it on top of some papers that looked like printed emails. She didn't say anything about the book, just rummaged further into her bag, complaining that she should never have brought her work bag to the parents' conference on Friday. The cookies she had taken as a snack for me were all crunched up, and had covered everything with brown cream.

Anyway, I need to focus on the good feeling so it doesn't disappear. So, what happened was that while Mom was emptying the bag Saturday morning, the beep went off in my ear! I stopped what I was doing so I could follow its directions. The beep works a bit like a radar, or like those games I played when I was younger, when Mom would hide something for me, and then say "hot" when I got closer, and "cold" when I moved away from it. Likewise, the beep gets louder when I move towards whatever is causing it, and fainter when I am further away.

I started moving away from the dining table, towards the kitchen, and the sound went quiet, but as I turned around and went back, the volume came back up. My heart started galloping, and when Mom asked for the fifth time if I wanted pancakes for breakfast, I had to shout at her to be quiet and not to disturb me. She got upset and just went into the kitchen, but I thought I could deal with her later, because now I really had to focus on what was making the beep so wild. And then my hands moved towards the book that Mom had put on the table. I picked it up and turned it around so I could see the title on the front, and the beep did a long, strong sound, and then it just settled in my heart, where it pulled out that amazing feeling which I told you was still in my body when I woke up this morning. I read the words of the title of the book, and it was as if I had eyes in my heart, as if I could look from my heart, and the book was luminous. It was light.

The room was spinning and I had to sit down, and I was just holding the book, and I felt I loved Mom so much, and I knew that even though she didn't talk to me about it, she also cared about the light. She had been carrying around in her bag a book that was full of light. She was probably reading it on the metro on her way to work. Or even in her lunch break.

I opened the book on a random page, and I could hardly believe what I was reading. It was about a radiance coming from a place which the author knew nothing about. I remember the word. Radiance. Then he called it Light. He told me he found light and joy at the same moment. He could only find them and lose them together.

This book proves that I am not crazy! It tells me that I am on to something, something that I haven't made up, or which is only a "response to difficult circumstances," as Mr. Finnley told Mom at the parents' conference on Friday. Unfortunately I cannot talk to the person who wrote this book, because he is dead. But if there once was someone like him, more people like that must exist.

I sat on my bed reading the book the whole of yesterday. I don't understand everything, but the words open that soft spot in my heart, and I feel real, and the world feels real. It is as if the man who wrote those words were talking directly to me, because I can feel him through those words. Even though he is dead, I can feel him, the way he was, and the kind of light that came through him.

I apologized to Mom for shouting at her about the pancakes, and explained the situation. She shrugged it off and said it was not nice to shout at someone, regardless of a beep in the ear. She was tired and did not want a drama. She fixed breakfast and went back to bed to rest. Which was a good thing, really, as it gave me the whole day to read.

Mom said that someone at work had given her the book as a present, and that she had looked at it, but she didn't feel too good about this religious friend of hers trying to convert her. "I am not desperate," she said. "I am keeping it real, seeing things for what they are, accepting the limitations of the human body. I am not turning to religious fantasy in order to run away from my fears."

I have decided that I will read some pages from this book for Mom every day. I will tell her that she can rest, and I will read for her. I started last night. She looked at me after I had read the first chapter, and her eyes were alive, and I felt that flash in my heart that tells me that we feel each other from the inside. It's funny, Mom used to read for me every evening when I was smaller, and now I am reading for her.

I want to tell you a bit about the man who wrote this book full of shiny words. I would like you to read it, as I am pretty sure you would love it too. Maybe you can buy the book as well, and we can read it at the same time, you, Mom and I.

Anyway, the author is someone called Jacques Lusseyran. I looked him up on the Internet. When he was seven, he had an accident at school. His glasses broke and ripped his eyes. When he woke up, he was totally blind. But the strange thing is that this accident did not make him sad! He says that being blind made him happier, made it possible for him to see light everywhere, and that he only felt despair when he was looking in the wrong direction... which happened when he was scared.

I want to understand this.

I wish I had someone to talk to about these things.

I mean, apart from you.

Someone who understands them better than I do.

Wet Turtles

Washington, D.C., USA, November 2007

I have met the neighbor!

The one with all the strange things stored in the attic.

It happened yesterday. I spoke to him. I sat in his kitchen drinking a cup of rosehip tea.

It was raining, and he must have been the only person outside in the bad weather. I sat warm in bed with my duvet around me, watching him lean into the wind as he snail-walked along the fence, his beard flapping like a white flag, and his black clothes glued to him. He wore a dark cap on his head when he started walking. About halfway down the first lane, a really strong gust of wind lifted the cap off his head, twirled it around in the air, and landed it in the Oak tree on our side of the fence. My body recognized this for what it was: an invitation to run down into the garden, climb the tree, get that cap, jump into the neighbor's yard, and hand it back to him. So I did all of this, before my brain had a chance to interfere. My turtle slippers got all wet and slimy. But that was OK. Because it was the right thing to do.

When I handed him his cap, I couldn't help but stare at him, because he looked so different close up. I could never make out his face or see his eyes clearly from my window. He looked younger than I had imagined. His eyes were sparkly and very blue.

You have blue eyes as well, Dad, right?

Mom sometimes tells me that I have your eyes. If that is so, we must be seeing the same kind of things.

Standing in front of him made me feel all wobbly inside. A strong beep came in my ear. I found it hard to say anything. When he asked me if I wanted to come inside and have a cup of tea, I just nodded because I knew to trust the beep.

I followed him through the brambly garden and into his house. He asked if I liked rosehip tea. I had never had it before, so I said yes.

His house was nothing like the houses of my friends. Everything looked really old. I say everything, but there wasn't much. The kitchen had an old sink, a stove, and a painted blue, wooden table, with two blue chairs without cushions on them. The walls were yellowish, and there were paintings without frames hanging everywhere. Some were of nature scenes. Trees, mountains, lakes. Some were signs or images that I couldn't tell what they were. There was one brown mug turned upside down next to the sink, and on the stove sat an old-looking kettle in which he boiled the water for the rosehip tea. The kettle made a whistling noise when the water started boiling. He poured the water over a teabag in a mug with flags from many different countries on it. Then he asked, "One or two sugars?"

I didn't know what to say, as I don't really drink much tea, so I just answered, "Two please!"

A twig had scratched my face when I jumped into his yard, and there must have been a bit of blood. He took out some cotton wool and antiseptic cream from one of the cupboards, and put it on the scratch. He said he didn't have any Band-Aids, but if I kept the cotton wool there, it would stop bleeding.

The house had a kind of sweet and musty smell, and it was so silent. In a good way, like you can find in the forest. I held the cotton wool on my face, and drank the hot tea, which was very sweet and delicious. Sitting there with him made me happy in a very quiet way. I could feel and see the kind of light there was in the neighbor, and I could also feel that there was not much fear inside of him.

I can normally see the kind of fear that is inside people, particularly in adults. In kids the fear tends to come, and then leave after a short while, whereas in adults the fear may stay for so long that it becomes a thick shell. Then it is almost impossible to see what kind of light they have, or to feel any life moving in them.

The neighbor seemed unusual to me. He was sort of empty, but not empty like a cup before the tea is poured, more like completely full-empty, if that makes sense. Warm, full, sweet, empty, and with clear light. Our conversation in the kitchen went a little bit like this:

"You like the tea?"

"Yes, I do."

"Good climbing!"

"Thanks!"

"Your turtles are wet."

"That's OK."

"Has it stopped bleeding?"

"Yes."

"So you watch me walk?"

"You know?"

"Yes."

"Don't you get bored by walking the same path so slowly?"

"No. Don't you get bored watching me?"

"Yes and no. You're like a walking tree."

"You like trees!"

"I do."

"You can take the easy route home. The Oak is too slippery."

"Yes."

Then he took me to the front door, and we said goodbye, and I went back to check on Mom. She had not noticed I was gone, and asked me to set the table, so I did. She did not even see the scratch.

Thanksgiving

Washington, D.C., USA, Thanksgiving Day, 2007

Good morning! Good morning! Wherever you are, Dad, Good morning!

I'm sorry I have been sounding gloomy lately. Today I am writing to you with my happy sweater on. I wear this blue furry sweater on special days, and today is the perfect day for wearing it.

It is Thanksgiving, and we are having turkey. (Mom said there was no point in buying a whole turkey for only the two of us, so she got a breast.)

I love when the house is glowing and alive with delicious, homey smells from the kitchen. She doesn't cook very often, because she is always too tired, but today she has energy, and I am so happy.

There was a storm last night. Many branches were torn off by the strong wind. The streets and gardens are littered with wood. Some of our neighbors had their power lines cut by big trees falling. Our breakfast room, or the sun room as I call it, has a big branch from my best Oak tree on the roof.

Do you celebrate Thanksgiving, Dad? I guess you probably don't because you are not in America, and it's only here that we celebrate the arrival of the pilgrims. Pilgrims are different from trees. Pilgrims keep walking to a holy place. Trees don't need to walk to get there.

The New World of the pilgrims didn't prove very good for the Native Americans, though.

Perhaps when you think that all the earth beneath your feet, wherever you go, is already holy, like I have read Native Americans do, then maybe you walk differently on it, and treat it differently, or you stop feeling the need to walk so fast, like a tree, and you can be still. I wonder if the neighbor feels more like a pilgrim or a tree. He certainly walks a lot, like the pilgrims. But he walks so slowly, so he is also like a tree.

Mom says it is important to be grateful for life.

I am grateful. I feel grateful that I can write to you, and that today is a calm and warm morning. I feel grateful to have found the book Mom was carrying around. The fact that she is well enough to make turkey today is another thing that I am grateful for. And then there is something new and surprising that I really need to tell you about.

After lunch Mom wanted to rest, so I tidied up. We had left half of the pumpkin pie. I wrapped cling film over the pie and placed it in the fridge next to the elderflower cordial.

I love elderflower cordial. It reminds me of summer and of sitting under the big tree in Sigrid's garden.

The Lump Broke Free

Washington, D.C., USA, Thanksgiving Friday 2007

The day after Thanksgiving Mom still wanted to take it easy so she stayed in her room watching a movie. I was downstairs alone and started feeling bored. I tried reading but my mind was all jumpy so I couldn't concentrate. I searched through the kitchen cupboards and found a packet of madeleines, which I ate. I opened the fridge and forgot why I had opened it and stood there holding the open fridge door with my right hand, staring at the milk, sausages and yogurts. I felt the cold from the fridge on my legs and my tummy and missed Norway. I imagined Mom catching me staring into the fridge, shouting at me to close the door before the penguins escaped. Thinking penguins lived in the fridge usually made me chuckle and had me close the door, but now, instead of closing the fridge I reached for the leftover pie from yesterday. And for the bottle of elderflower cordial.

I put the pie and the bottle in a brown paper bag, got my boots on, and opened the door as quietly as I could. It was cold outside, but I walked quickly the few steps over to the neighbor's front door. I rang the bell. There was no sound, so I thought it probably did not work. I had never seen him open the door to anyone. Sometimes the odd sales person would ring the bell, wait for a while, then walk off.

I wondered if he might be thinking I was a sales person, or somebody asking for money or work, like tidying up his yard, or trimming the trees, and that he just would not open the door. Come to think about it, he definitely would not open the door, as he did not know that it was me standing there with pumpkin pie and elderflower cordial.

I did not want to go back home without having had a chance to see him again.

I started knocking on the door, repeating, "Walking Tree, Walking Tree, it's me!"

After what felt like a very long time, I heard someone behind the door. A lock made a clicking sound, and the door swung open. He looked at me without smiling this time. I looked back, and my insides got jelly again. "Pumpkin pie and elderflower cordial," I said in a small voice. "You want some?"

He didn't answer straight away, and I felt my heart beating. I tried to smile.

"Come on in," he said, and I followed him through the dark hallway and into a living room which was at the opposite side to the kitchen. An old and worn-looking red corduroy sofa was placed against the wall, with a painting on a canvas without a frame above it, of hills and a lake. A small dark, wooden coffee table stood in front of the sofa, with a brown leather arm chair on the other side, a tall lamp next to it, surrounded by piles and piles of books. The stacks of books seemed to be used as little tables, with empty tea mugs on several of them. Scribbled notes floated on top of the books. There was also a wooden desk with a chair, covered with more books and papers. Next to the desk was a small, old-looking TV. There were no mats on the floor, only scratched, worn wooden floorboards. I sat down on the red sofa. It was soft and low, and it swallowed me up as I sank deep into it.

I put the pie and the elderflower cordial on the coffee table.

He left the room.

I was hoping he went to the kitchen to fetch plates and glasses.

I looked at a drawing hanging on the wall above the armchair. A Native American chief with lots of feathers on his head.

He came back with plates and glasses. And this time what we said was something like this:

"Elderflower drink… Haven't had that since I was a boy."

"That's a long time."

"My Mom used to make it. Back home."

"I had it back home too."

"Not such a long time."

"Do you know any Indians?"

"No."

"Not even the one on the wall?"

"No."

"I used to drink elderflower cordial with ice cubes in the summer with my friend."

"No need for ice cubes today."

And as we sat drinking, I had a feeling which I recognized from the summers with Sigrid. That nothing was complicated. If I just focused on the taste of the drink, and on the pie, and on the neighbor across from me, then everything was simple, and it felt good in my whole body, like honey.

Then we continued talking:

"Why do you walk so slowly in your yard?"

"It puts what was split up back together."

"Does it make light?"

"Yes."

"OK."

"Mom is sick. Would slow walking help?"

"Depends on how split up she is."

"A lot. Her cells are dividing, without stopping."

"Cancer?"

"In the lungs."

He just looked at me, and the way he looked at me made me feel like all the things I had been trying so hard not to feel, the fear and the sadness, and the anger… Mom sick… It was all there, in the space between my body and his.

"It's OK," he said.

And then, I tried to swallow that big lump in my throat with an extra big sip of elderflower cordial but it went down the wrong way, and the lump broke free and there was water coming out of my eyes, and out of my mouth, and I was coughing, and

I couldn't breathe, and then it felt like there were aliens in my body, pushing up from my tummy, through my chest and out of my mouth, and they were making an awful noise, like howling. And he just sat there very calmly.

And then he said, "It is all right. It can come out. It's all right. It can come out."

And as the aliens left my body, it started feeling more like waves crashing against the shore inside me, sometimes getting hold of me, washing me out to sea, and I went under, and I couldn't sense where dry land was anymore, and I tried to swim, but it was not working, and then I got washed up on the shore again, and somehow the waves stopped, and there was stillness. And there was light.

"I am glad you came to see me today."

"Yes."

Then we sat there for a while longer without saying anything. Then I felt it was time to go.

"Can I come to see you again?"

"Yes, you can."

He walked me through the dark hallway. I put my boots on, and we said goodbye.

The Ex-actress's Cat

Washington, D.C., USA, Same Friday, November 2007

I walked back from the neighbor, feeling floaty and light after having had all that water come out of my eyes. I wanted to go home and lie down as I felt dizzy, but I put my hands in my pockets and a key slipped into my fingers. Brandon! I had forgotten about him.

Brandon is a cat who belongs to the ex-actress. Every day she takes him for a walk in a blue stroller, like the one you would expect to see a small child in. She strolls down the block, goes to the little park, takes Brandon out of the stroller, lets him sniff around the grass for five minutes, while holding his leash, then she puts him back into the stroller and takes him home.

Jennifer had agreed to cat sit while the owner, the ex-actress, was out of town. This is because she is the official helper on our block. But in my opinion, Jennifer takes on too much: watching me, arranging block parties, looking out for old Mrs. Higgins, being on the local council committee, and cat sitting for the ex-actress. She is not happy about the cat sitting, as Brandon is not an ordinary cat, more like a human baby, but Jennifer cannot say no to anyone who needs her. Anyway, she had promised but then realized she was also going away. And so she passed the double booking on to me. I forgot to take Brandon out yesterday, so although I really wanted to go home, I felt guilty and went over to his house.

Now, it must be clear to everyone, except to the ex-actress, that Brandon is deeply depressed. He doesn't show much interest in anything around him. In the past I have tried to take him around the park, introduce him to other cats, throw toy mice at him, put him high up in trees, place him in the sandpit, but nothing works. He just stands there staring into space. I know he is a house cat, but seriously, how can a cat be so out of touch with his instincts. Maybe he is on drugs or something, although the ex-actress told Jennifer it's a normal response to missing his mommy. She usually walks past my house with the stroller every day. I have tried to say hello, but she ignores me. She wears dark sunglasses and high heels. The kind of platform high heels, and she is the skinniest lady I have ever seen. Maybe she had to be skinny to get work as an actress. Jennifer says she almost made it in Hollywood, and once played in a movie that was meant to have Johnny Depp in it, except he pulled out last minute. The movie was about aliens that looked like dogs trying to take over America. The ex-actress played the love interest who fell in love with the main alien dog, and had to be rescued by the hero, not played by Johnny. It was a flop, and after that she only did commercials, until that stopped as well, and now she is an ex-actress, writing a book that will make her famous. At least that is what Jennifer told me.

I walked up the block, unlocked the door, went inside the ex-actress's small, dark living room, and called for Brandon. The blinds were down and I fumbled to find the light switch. There were thick carpets on the floor and the smell of cigarettes was strong. Brandon was curled up on a purple, velvety sofa. He lifted his head and glared at me. "Walkies!" I tried, but he disappeared into an adjoining bedroom. Clearly not happy to see me, nor excited about his daily stint in the stroller. I felt exhausted and did not want to chase Brandon. I sat down on the sofa and looked around.

There was a liquor cabinet on one side of the room. Next to the sofa was a small table with an ashtray shaped like a frog, and an old CD player, the kind I remember Mom let me play with back in Norway as nobody used it anymore. Janis Joplin's *Cheap Thrills* was on the floor. I put the CD in and pressed play. The music sounded old fashioned, but I quite liked something in her voice. I imagined the ex-actress taking a break from writing her book, smoking a cigarette, drinking red wine, and dancing around in her platform shoes, with Janis shouting *baby, baby* a lot and that someone was taking a piece of her heart. Still feeling rather floaty and not quite myself, I opened the liquor cabinet. There was an opened bottle of red wine. I removed the top and poured some into a dirty glass left on the table. I sipped the wine. It tasted like vinegar. I took another sip. Then I remembered Brandon and felt guilty again, so I went to look for him in the bedroom. He was nowhere to be seen. But there was a dark blue, silk dressing gown with golden stars draped on the bed and three pairs of platform shoes on the floor. I put on the dressing gown, slipped my feet into a yellow pair of platforms. It felt good to be hovering high above the ground. I walked back to the living room with Janis still roaring, and the dressing gown swiping the carpet. I picked up the glass, swayed and jumped and sipped the wine, thinking this had to be how the ex-actress felt on her writing breaks.

I am telling you this, because Mom would not understand about wanting to pretend to be someone else for a while. And also because Janis started screaming about being alone and calling for her Daddy, and she was just screaming *no, no, no* a lot, and then she was calling for the *Lord* or what have you... and that she was sitting there all alone and was wondering where her Daddy was... and that she kept searching for him, and I'm not sure who it was she had left, but that she regretted leaving... And the song went on like that for a long time, with Janis sounding more and more crazy, and although I didn't think much of the song, I got into the feeling of it, and the vinegar wine didn't taste so bad any more, and I was imagining Johnny Depp parking outside, coming in, telling me, or the ex-actress, how much he regretted not taking that part in the movie about the alien dogs, and... and then my phone rang, and I saw it was Jennifer's number, so I turned off the music and picked it up.

The rest of the story is embarrassing. The ex-actress had

just called Jennifer, shouting at the top of her voice that she had trusted her with the care of her darling baby (whom I now realized was called Brando) and what was going on with that strange child from down the street going crazy in her living room?!? Jennifer sounded more hysterical than I had ever heard her, screaming at me to be normal for once, and not to do those stupid things.

It turns out that this ex-actress's friend had walked past with his dog, seen the lights on, and decided to peek in through the window. He had watched my live performance and called the ex-actress.

I quickly left the house without letting Brando out, hoping Jennifer wouldn't call Mom.

The Hospital

Washington, D.C., USA, the Saturday after Thanksgiving, November 2007

When I woke up my tummy was aching, and I had to run to the bathroom. I felt sick and scared.

Once out of the bathroom, my feet wanted to take me to Mom's room, but my tummy got more tense as I approached the staircase, so I stopped. The house was quiet. Not quiet in the way of the neighbor's house. This was a kind of quiet that made me all tense.

Have you ever noticed how many kinds of quiet there are in the world? This was a kind of quiet that you might feel in a creepy kind of playground or park where you would expect to hear birds singing, but for some reason the birds know that it's not a happy place, so they just keep quiet.

I forced myself to walk up the stairs, and paused again outside Mom's room.

I whispered, "Mom, are you awake?"

She did not answer.

I opened the door and went in as carefully as I could, so as not to wake her up in case she was having a good sleep.

She had her eyes closed. Her face was very white, yellowy white, and it looked more scrawny than ever, as if something had been gobbling on her cheeks from the inside during the night. She was breathing in a way that told me it was not easy to be her. Like she had to use all her strength just to breathe.

Touched her face. Felt cold and damp.

Said in a strange, loud voice, "Mom, are you OK?"

Knew she was not OK... stupid question.

Shook her by the shoulder, she did not respond.

Picked up her cell phone from the table next to her bed. Could see an unanswered call, and a text message from Jennifer on the home screen. Mom had not seen it.

Phone was locked. Didn't know her PIN number.

Ran into my room to find my phone. Wasn't allowed to use it much, only have it with me when outside, so she knew she could always reach me.

Hadn't used it for many days. Flat battery.

Started panicking. Looked everywhere for charger. Mom wouldn't buy me the same kind of nice phone she had. Felt very angry with Mom for not buying me a better phone. Have an old and ugly phone.

Could have used her charger if we had the same kind.

No charger anywhere. No time to look for it.

Mom said nobody used landlines at home any more. Stupid, stupid, stupid. Landlines don't need chargers.

Ran downstairs, out of the house, knocked on the neighbor's door again, shouted, "Open, open, open, it's me!"

He came quickly this time. I shouted, "Your phone, your phone! Mom is sick!" He nodded and we went into the living room. The plates and the glasses from my visit were still on the table. He removed some papers covering an old-looking phone sitting on his desk. He still had a landline. I grabbed the receiver and hit the numbers 911 so hard that my finger hurt. He followed me back into the house. We waited for the ambulance. He followed me into the ambulance. We sat there in silence. He followed me into the hospital.

I imagine that if you had been living with us, you would have been holding my hand as the ambulance whizzed through the familiar streets on our way to the hospital. You also would have seen the few cars driving on the Saturday after Thanksgiving stop to let us through. Do you know that when you are inside the ambulance the siren is not as loud as I had imagined? Still, it was loud enough. The "nee-naw, nee-naw, nee-naw" went into my ears in a way that made it feel like everything was made of sound. But this was not like the beep I normally have in my ear, the beep that alerts me of the light. This sound called forth the dark. And it was not a luminous dark. Only dark. And Mom was in it. And I was in it. I know that the author of the book I told you about, the one about light, says that despair is simply the matter of looking the wrong way, and that the light only fades when afraid. I did not know how to look the right way as I was sitting there with Mom on my way to the hospital.

Felt a dry, warm hand touch my hand. Opened my hand and put it in the palm of the neighbor.

He gave me a rope to hold on to as the darkness washed over me.

And he was still holding my hand as we sat waiting on a hard, black leather couch in the hospital. Felt cold, forgot my jacket. They had rolled Mom somewhere, and told us to wait. It was a place for waiting. Waiting to hear something, waiting to hear something about people making it to dry land… that they were only cold and needed rest… terrified of hearing that they had swallowed too much water, or were freezing beyond heating up, or that their lungs were too wet to carry air.

Had a floaty sense of being on a boat. Could not really feel my feet. They seemed to be made of air. Could see my body sitting and waiting, but I was not really in there, in my body. The only place on my body still warm was my hand, which the neighbor held in his. It was like an anchor stopping me from drifting to the ceiling like a balloon. A nurse came out and smiled at us. She said that Mom needed to stay. I knew that already. The only problem, no babysitter during the Thanksgiving holiday. I have already told you that Jennifer and Katherine were away.

Went home in a taxi cab with the neighbor. Don't remember much from the drive. Was still suspended in the dark place, looking for Mom. Knew she was in there somewhere, but could not find her. Knew that if I stopped looking for her, she might get lost in there forever, and never come back. Knew it was my job to rescue her from that dark sea and to make sure that she would come back from the hospital.

Had to concentrate really hard. The neighbor asked if I wanted to bring some of my stuff over to his house and sleep in the second bedroom. Nodded and picked up a blanket and the rock that I had painted for Mom. She kept it on her bedside table. The rock has glitter on it and a dragonfly. Mom knows that I have put my love in that rock and that she should always keep it with her.

She usually would put it in her bag when she went to the hospital. Now the rock was here, and she was there. Went back to the neighbor again. Was beginning to get used to walking through his door.

He showed me the second bedroom. Put my rock on a chest of drawers by the door. There was only the single bed, a chest of drawers and more books. Didn't seem like anyone had stayed in there in a very, very long time. The room felt as in a deep slumber. Didn't really want to talk much, but asked him if there was a ladder to the attic somewhere. He said there was a pull-down ladder in the hallway. Asked if anyone was staying in the attic. He looked at me with a puzzled expression. "Nobody is staying in the attic," he said. "Then why are the lights on up there?" I asked. Thought I might as well be direct, "The voices... that come out late at night?"

First he looked blankly at me, as though he couldn't compute. Then he said, "It's a funny electrical set up in this old house. When I turn the lights on in my bedroom, it also switches on the lights in the attic. There's a lot of junk up there."

I just stared at him.

"I sometimes have trouble sleeping, and listen to the radio in bed. Perhaps that's what you've heard. I also have people in faraway places call me late at night. Sometimes I talk to them. I won't do that tonight. I'll keep quiet so you can sleep."

Heard what he said. Part of me believed that he was telling

the truth, part of me was still remembering the images in my head about what went on in his attic. All the body parts and hairs and nurses and lost animals…

He sat down on the edge of my bed and looked at me with calm eyes.

Decided my doubts had to wait. He was all I had to hold on to. Still floating in the dark. Needed to concentrate on Mom.

Said, "OK." Asked, "What is your name?"

"Garrick."

Fell asleep and dreamt about bodies in the sea all night. Was looking for Mom in the dark water. You know she is not a good swimmer. Bodies everywhere. And we were there, with all the arms and legs and feet and hands and heads and eyes. Hoping a boat would come along. Had lost Mom. Had to find her, among the arms and the feet and the heads and the legs, had to find Mom. Needed to swim with her on my back. Woke up a few times, sweating and waving my arms. Drifted back to sea, with the arms and the eyes and the feet.

Woke up with the light outside. Was sitting on a stranded raft, on a beach somewhere unknown. Foreign land. Was listening for sounds of the neighbor moving around, but couldn't hear anything. Couldn't remember what day it was. Was it a school day? Went over to the window and looked out. Could see our house from this foreign land. Could see the window of my room. It looked like a blind eye. Could see that the house was holding its breath, waiting. Felt seasick. Still floaty. Had to keep very still not to lose my balance and fall over.

Writing all of this down helps. It helps me stay on dry land. And when you read it, you will know exactly how it was this day when Mom went to the hospital.

Floating in the Dark Sea

Washington, D.C., USA, the Sunday after Thanksgiving. November 2007

Went downstairs to look for the neighbor. Remembered that he was called Garrick (not a name I had heard before). He was in the kitchen drinking a cup of tea, reading a newspaper.

The black rolling bag was parked next to his chair. He looked up as I entered. He said nothing, but his eyes told me that he was making a space for me to say something if I wanted to.

"You didn't go out last night at 6.30pm, as you often do," I blurted.

Looked towards his black bag.

"I did go out. To the hospital. With you," he said and pulled out a chair for me. "Would you like some porridge... oats?"

Don't normally have oats for breakfast, but said, "Yes, please." Garrick got up to stir the pot.

The porridge tasted of sawdust. Wet sawdust, but didn't mind. Thought that I was lucky I had been picked up from the sea, brought to dry land and given porridge. All those bodies still floating, Mom still lost at sea, and me on land eating porridge...

Called the hospital and asked about Mom. They said she was sleeping, but she was doing better. I could come and see her in the afternoon if I wanted.

It was 8am when I called. The afternoon seemed far away.

Garrick went in to the living room and sat down in his armchair with a book.

I sat down on the red sofa, or more like, I was half swallowed by the red sofa, and we made a small conversation:

"Do you like reading?"

"Yes."

"What are you reading?"

"A book about a man who was blind but could see light."

"What is it called?"

"I don't remember. But it is good. It's more of an adult book, but I don't mind. I read it anyway."

"Hum."

"I used to feel good just thinking of that book... but now it doesn't work anymore…"

"…"

"Mom says you were in the Vietnam War."

"Yes. I was."

"Where do you go at night?"

"To the shelter. I am a volunteer."

"Shelter?"

"For the homeless. Night shifts three times a week. I should go there tonight as well. But I will change my shifts."

"Do you think I'm strange?"

"Yes," he said, and continued reading his book.

I sat staring into space.

I went back to my house to get some food from the fridge, my book, and clean clothes.

It felt like sadness was waiting for me in the hallway, waiting to pounce on me, cling to me as soon as I put my foot inside. Like thick fog or mist seeping into my body, making me feel heavy and gray. I found the book in my room. Opened it and tried to read, but the sadness was affecting my eyesight, and I couldn't really focus on the words.

It's funny how it's easier to write than to read when upset. I find that when I'm writing to you, imagining that you see what I see, and feel what I feel, then my eyesight clears up a little.

I went outside in the garden. Sat next to my thorny tree. The tree took away most of the mist in me. I could see more clearly. The leaves, the birds, the little acorns on the ground. The roly-polies that I loved to play with when I was younger. I picked one up and it instantly rolled itself into a tight ball. Then it realized it was safe and started walking again. I thought about the neighbor and went back to his house with the food.

He was not inside. He had left the door open so I could get in. I went into the kitchen to put the food down, and as I glanced out of the kitchen window, I could see him in the back yard. He was doing his snail-walking. This was unusual. He had broken the rhythm of his "poem." He always did his snail-walking much later. I had disturbed the rhythm of his day. I went out and sat down on a dry tree stub to watch him. He didn't look up when I arrived, just continued his walk, or glide.

It was different watching him so close up. I could feel him as I watched him, and as I felt him, I also felt myself relaxing a little. I wondered why it was that I could feel some people, and others I could not feel at all. I wondered where they really were when I couldn't feel them, and whether they lived in a world where they did not feel themselves or other people, or trees or anything. I found that a scary thought, because if they could not feel me or anyone else, they might treat me, and other people, say their daughters or students or the refugees, just like things, just like other things that they could not feel. It doesn't really matter much what we do to things, like destroy them or drop them, or store them. Or chop them down.

Then I decided to get up and try snail-walking myself. I stood up and placed myself behind him. Not so close as to disturb him, but not so far away that I couldn't feel him. And then I copied him. I snail-walked behind him. I disappeared into his rhythm, like I imagine you will do with my words when reading this. I tried to put my foot down when he did, and to keep my balance. It's not so easy to walk this slowly. You have to become aware of every part of your body, and not think of anything else, because if you start thinking about other things then you might lose your balance, or speed up.

First I felt like my head was going to explode, and there was fog covering everything. But as I kept walking behind him, the fog lifted, and it was like I disappeared and became more solid and present at the same time. And believe it or not, the beep was there, and we were making light. Or maybe we didn't make it, maybe it was always there, we just couldn't see it, I don't know, but as we walked together, I saw and felt the light again. The beep in my ear, and then the light was back. Even with Mom in the dark, the light was back. I kept walking. I could see the world from inside his walk. Everything looked different from here. So much space, and silence, and light in this walk. I was everywhere, and what was me was just space and light... and it was coming through my body.

I don't know for how long we walked. Time stopped. There was peace at that place where time was not.

When we stopped he looked at me for a long time, and I know he saw me.

He looked stern, but not unfriendly, just like someone might look at another person with whom they have just shared something that is hard to describe, but you know is very close to something that is true or real, and the last thing you would care about is putting your face back into a mask for other people to like, and see you only from the "outside." Not that Garrick did that anyway. He didn't seem to care about how other people saw him. I tried to look back at him from the place in me that I knew he was looking into, which was not the place that I normally think of as "me." I could have been as old as him, or he could have been as young as me. It reminded me of being hugged by the Saint, when the electrons collapsed into the center of the atom. Do you remember that I told you about that? You are the only person I have ever told about the electrons and the atom and the Saint. Mom would not understand. I might try to tell Garrick. But I would prefer if I could talk to you about it.

When we sat in the kitchen and drank our rosehip tea after the walk, I asked him where he had learned to do that. He told me that during his time in Vietnam he had become so split up inside from the things he had seen and done, that he had found it hard to imagine any future for himself.

He had met a person who had saved his life, he said. Taken him to a Buddhist monastery, where he had stayed for five years. With the help of the people there, the meditation and the slow walking, he started to become less split up.

I asked if he still felt split up sometimes.

"Yes, I do," he said. "We get flung apart... and then we have to find our way back, again, and again... to wholeness... and hopefully stay a bit longer for each time we enter back. My body never forgets, though. It comes out at night, in dreams and sweats."

He was quiet while we sipped the tea. I didn't know what else to say to him. He spoke to me as if I were an adult and a real person, not a child. I liked that. I wished he would go on talking. I remembered finding the magazine in Sigrid's house that day when I heard her mom talking to the other man on the phone. The magazine that had made my beep go so crazy when I read about the light and the poet being crushed. I wondered if the neighbor was talking about something similar.

"Everything affects everything else," he said eventually. "We cannot take ourselves out of the picture... we are a part of it. What I did to others during the war, I also did to myself... Human beings are not clever machines or things... nature is not a thing where we can dump our useless stuff. Nothing ever disappears." He looked at me to see if I understood. I nodded my head, because I wanted him to keep talking.

"The mirror broke a long time ago," he muttered. "The atom isn't the only thing that splits... we split too...crack like glass, because we are in there...in the picture, in that mirror... splitting off from who we truly are, from what makes us human... and then nothing really matters any more... So it becomes easy to treat each other like things... Because you understand, materialism... and should I say fundamentalism, give us a world where nothing really holds together. Our puny minds cannot hold it all together… It splits everything into millions of things that we can label and study and control and make into rights and wrongs... taking us further away from what is whole and holy."

I looked at him, and as he talked I felt the same kind of pull that kept me watching him from my window.

"What is it that can hold it all together?'" he asked.

"I don't know," I said.

"What is it to you?" he insisted.

My mind was blank. There was a big gap. Then I felt hot, and words came into my mouth, "It is what keeps the electrons spinning."

His body went very still, and he cocked his head to the right. "What is that?" he said with surprise.

"What keeps the electrons spinning…" I said again. "Is love," I whispered.

He was quiet. Sipped his tea.

I didn't know whether I had said something stupid or not. He did not say a word.

I waited. But still he kept silent.

Then I said, "Do you think that nature is sick because of us humans? And if we are part of nature... and Mom is sick…"

I found it hard to make long sentences that connected the different things we were talking about, because my brain didn't really understand all of it.

I managed to add, "Mr. Finnley talks about climate change a lot. He says that some people don't believe in it."

Garrick leaned forward and put his cup down on the table. He looked out of the window and said in a voice that sounded annoyed, "Well... everything has a price, hasn't it? Consumerism has a price… It has us believe we were born lacking… If only we buy another car or a bigger house, produce more useless stuff… than we will one day fill that unbearable emptiness inside... and in the meantime forests are dying and the seas are filling up with plastic. You know about all of this! Kids know this better than adults. We have to rely on you all being smarter than us, that you don't forget what you know as you grow up. You don't want to lose your soul, live a trivial life, do you?"

"Trivial?" I asked, scared that I would interrupt his flow of words, but also wanting to understand.

"Trivial... well... I guess I'm using the word to mean superficial or insignificant... in mathematics I believe it is relating to being the solution of an equation in which every variable is equal to zero. All the materialism in the world, without a connection to anything bigger than itself, ultimately equals to zero." He said this all in one go, and I stared at him.

"Trivial," I repeated.

"Yes," he said, looking straight at me.

I do not want to be trivial. Have my life equal to zero.

He sounded so serious when he spoke of those things, and I got a bit scared.

"I'm happy that science can help your Mom now, of course I am! But I also think we need to keep connected to our true nature, and to nature itself... call it soul if you want. If not, we become scared and confused in times of crisis. We become stupid when we are too rational and forget that nature and symbols can hold it all together. Do you know what a symbol is?" he asked.

"I think so," I said. I felt the knot in my stomach tense up as he had mentioned Mom being sick. "In the book I'm reading it says that everything in the world is a sign for something else. And I remember Miss Green, my English teacher, saying that symbols are signs for something else, and I think she said they can make us learn about things that might be even invisible," I heard myself answer.

He took a deep breath, and kind of shrugged, like a dog shaking water off from his fur. Then he said, "What you said about the love and the atom and the electrons... I like that symbol."

A gush of relief spurted through my heart.

We sat quiet, and the peacefulness of the house caught up with us.

When he started talking again, his voice was softer. "Perhaps the old Hindu philosophers were right, saying the world history goes through cycles from a golden age to one of darkness, in which everything is chaos and turmoil. The point is that the wheel will always eventually turn, and humanity will renew itself..." He took a big sip of tea, and I did the same. "It's all very well in the long term, isn't it?" he said, looking at me with a smile. "And in the meantime, we have to do our best to swim against the tide, and not give up. To give way to despair is the ultimate cop-out, don't you agree?"

I didn't say anything.

"My guess is that we're in the same business, you and me, Luna. And we must not give in to despair. Even if it is difficult."

It was like being in a lesson where I had to pay attention to everything. I did not miss a word. I thought it might take a long time for me to really understand what we were talking about and my brain to catch up. But he had said that we were in the same business. I wanted to be in the same business as him, even if I didn't know what that was.

I wrote all of this down as well as I could, so you can see for yourself the strange ways in which he talks. Not how most people talk, right?

I was so exhausted after our chat that I went up to the guest room and curled up in bed. I slept really deeply, and when I woke up it was time to go and see Mom.

I brought Mom's painted rock, the book I was reading, and Garrick to the hospital.

As I entered the hospital, I could feel the ground under my feet a bit more than last time. I was no longer like a balloon in the air. My left hand touched the rock which I had in my pocket, and I was concentrating on seeing beautiful things around me, so that when I met Mom, she would feel some of that, and not just how scared and sad I was, which would not be very good for her.

There were flowers on the desk in the reception. A bouquet of yellow, white and red.

In the elevator there was nothing beautiful, so I looked at Garrick. I guess you wouldn't really call him beautiful, I mean to look at, but then I looked into his eyes, and there was beauty. Light blue, very clear, like the sky on a summer's day.

Then we arrived to her room. Garrick said he would wait outside.

Mom was sitting up in bed, leaning on big cushions, and I could see from her face that she had been waiting for me.

I stopped a little away from the bed. She looked so thin and pale, but also so lovely. Her hair seemed soft and her eyes were calm. She had the kind of eyes that she has when I know she is only focusing on me, and on nothing else. Not half-thinking about work, or the emails she needs to write while she is talking to me. I just wanted to stand there and look at her. I don't know why I couldn't walk up to her.

Then she reached out a hand, and my body bounced over to the bed faster than I could say "chocolate brownie." I hugged her. I wanted to climb up on the bed and lie on top of her, but I was scared that I would crush her. She must have felt the same way, because she signaled for me to climb into bed and to lie next to her, so I did, and we just lay there, holding each other. I had found her in that deep, dark water, I had found her among all the feet and heads and hands and grandmothers and kids and fathers and aunts and uncles and cousins in the water.

And I never wanted to let go of her.

I told her she had to meet the neighbor, Garrick, and I called for him. He was waiting just outside the door. He came in and smiled at Mom.

I learned that Mom had called Garrick while I was sleeping in the afternoon yesterday.

She told me Garrick had filled in some papers when we came to the hospital yesterday, and had left his address, phone number and also the number for his work. He had asked Mom to call him when she could.

Garrick said we were becoming good friends, and I confirmed it was true. She told me Jennifer and Katherine would be back from Florida on Friday. She also said she would let Mr. Finnley know that I might not be coming to school the next few days.

Then Garrick went outside again to give us some space.

Mom apologized for leaving me alone, and that I had to stay with Garrick. It was an emergency situation that should not have happened this way, she insisted. Yesterday someone from the hospital had called the shelter where Garrick works , and there they had confirmed that he had undergone a thorough police and background check, and was very well respected.

I said I was not at all worried about staying with him. Actually, considering how everything was difficult right now, Garrick was the best thing that had happened to me.

Then I didn't feel like talking any more, and Mom looked very weak, so I just held on to her, because I had found her in that deep, dark water.

And I never wanted to let her go.

As we were lying there, I remembered a song that Mom used to sing me when I was little. It's about a woman who is half-seal, half-human – a Selkie – who leaves her family to go back to the sea. So I started singing softly to Mom:

Child, come with me
To where the sun is made of gold
And the moon is a pearl.
We'll be sailing free
Let's go, you and me,
To where the sea meets our dreams.

Hear the thunder roll by
We will sail and we'll sing of the sea.

We floated in the dark sea together for what seemed like a long time. Staying there, keeping each other warm gave us strength.

When it felt like we were on dry land, I sat up and took out the rock from my pocket and put it on the bedside table. She said she had missed the rock, and was happy to have it next to her.

I also took out the book written by the man who could see light, and asked if she wanted me to read for her. She said that would be lovely, and I opened the book on a random page and started reading. About how he discovered that all things in the world have their own voice, and speak. Not in words, but in their own kind of way. Everything speaks: bookcases speak, sofas speak, shoes have things to say, and streets and the houses, too. Even silence speaks.

I looked up at Mom, to see if she understood, and her eyes were smiling. She glanced at the rock I had brought, and then back at me, and we both knew that we knew.

I continued reading, and Jacques told us how much he loved life, even at tough times, like fighting in a war, and going to a Nazi prison. He said that even at those times he never stopped loving life. And he said that even though it's easier to feel love when things are good, it is just as possible when things are bad.

I looked up at Mom again, and she patted my arm. She was still listening. I told her that light is like a mixture of water and air. And it flows, not like water, but in a much finer way. And it comes from everywhere and nowhere. Through me, Jacques spoke of a radiance that he could see in all things, like windows, clouds or a dog. And he said that we all can let light enter into us, become part of us. He said it was a bit like eating sunshine.

And I was trying to see the light in Mom's hospital bed when she stroked my hair. I stopped reading and enjoyed her hand touching me.

"Look how the sun creates patterns on the floor," Mom said.

I jumped off the bed, and pretended to scoop up some sunshine and brought it back to her. "Here you go, be a good Mommy and eat your sunshine," I laughed.

She pretended to slurp up the sunshine, but started coughing, and her eyes lost the light in them. I watched her cough, and it was as if someone had switched off the sunshine.

She leaned back, looked very white and weak. I asked if she wanted me to continue reading. She nodded, and Jacques went on to say that even darkness was made of light, only this light vibrated differently, like a slower kind of radiance.

I could feel my voice touching Mom's body, and I felt a tender attention from her. I felt that it is this kind of attention that makes it possible to see light everywhere. And I saw that the words I was reading, which were full of light, entered into her.

Then Jacques said that children always know more than they are able to tell, unlike adults who only know a tiny bit of what they say. And this is because children know things with their whole being, while adults know them only with their mind. This is also why when a child is not feeling well, she stops playing immediately and wants to be with her mother. (Jacques actually said *"his* mother," but I changed it to *"her* mother," so it sounded like he wrote it especially for me and Mom.)

I stopped reading. Mom had fallen asleep. Her head was turned slightly towards me. It appeared as if she was still looking at me through her closed eyes. I stroked her hair for a long time. It was soft. I wondered if she had brushed it herself, or if the nurse had brushed it.

Garrick came back, followed by a young nurse.

She said that Mom needed to sleep, and that I could come back tomorrow. She said they had contacted my uncle in Norway, but that he would not be able to fly over until next weekend.

"It's OK, she is staying with me," Garrick said.

Dad, I wish you could be here now.

On a Boat

Same day, 2007

I am sitting on my bed in Garrick's guest room. The walls are covered in faded, yellow wall paper. A wooden chair is placed underneath the window. I put my clothes on it at night. There is a large, heavy wardrobe made of dark wood, with carvings on the top, and a mirror covering the left door. There is no lampshade for the bulb hanging down from the ceiling in the middle of the room. This makes the light glary and too bright. A musty smell makes my nose go stuffy. The wallpaper underneath the window has large, dark stains, probably from rain coming in during tough storms. I didn't know what to do with myself, so I figured I'd write. It makes the time pass, and it helps with my messy feelings. It helps to have someone to talk to. So I write to you. Garrick talks to me, but I know he also likes to be quiet. Sometimes I have too many words, and they all come out very fast, so writing them down helps.

I like that my writing can make it possible for you to see and feel what I see and feel.

For example, on the metro back from the hospital, Garrick started talking about his travels. He asked me what my favorite way of traveling was, and I said I thought it might be by boat, although I haven't had much experience with boats, but that recently I have been particularly preoccupied with them. On BBC World News I have seen images of refugees in the sea, in small, crowded boats... and yet I always imagine it would be lovely to be on a sailing boat. Uncle Jakob has bought a sailing boat. Mom told me the other day that when we go to visit next time, we will go on his boat. I said to Mom that I couldn't wait for that to happen.

Garrick talked about how much he loved the ocean. Once he

had been on a boat for two months, with a friend, just sailing and fishing and sleeping and swimming. They had drifted from island to island in the archipelago east of Hanoi. Even spent a week at a floating village. He showed me some photographs of the two of them. In one photo Garrick, who looked very different without the long beard and with a young body, but with the same eyes, sat on the roof of a floating house, next to a dog. I asked how the dog got up there, and he said the dog was a master of climbing that roof, and that he sat there every evening. They became friends, Garrick and the dog, so he took to joining him on the roof in the evenings.

Garrick's sailor friend sold stuff. Pearls collected by his relatives, woven cloths, tea leaves, silk worms, chickens, either brought from the city to the villagers, or from the villagers to the city.

Garrick said he will always remember the feeling of those days on the sea. The softness of the mornings, the burning sun of noon, and the coolness of the starry nights. There was one storm while they were out, and he said he had been terrified of the sea while the storm raged.

I imagine you must be used to boats? I mean, since you are probably living on an island in Greece. Everyone has a boat there, right? I have seen images of beautiful fishing boats painted in blue and white.

Do you have a fishing boat?

Dad?

I tried very hard to think about the loveliness of Garrick's story. About the dog and him watching the stars together on the roof, and of Uncle Jakob's new sailing boat, and of not giving way to despair, but somehow my mind tricked me, and I ended up thinking of those refugees in the water again, and of Mom floating.

The Shelter

Washington, D.C., USA, the Monday after Thanksgiving, 2007

Monday morning Garrick said he had to go to work. He had been rearranging his schedule because of me, and they needed him at the shelter by 9:30am. He said he would be back around 6pm. I didn't want to go back to school yet. I didn't feel ready to be there and I'd only be worrying about Mom, trying to appear normal. But I didn't want to stay by myself either. Garrick said I could go with him and help out if I wanted to, until the afternoon when I would go and see Mom.

I thought about it for a little while, wondered what it might be like to spend the morning in the shelter. I had been curious about it. I decided to go with Garrick.

We took a bus to the metro station, and then we took the red line downtown.

Once we got to our stop, we had a long way to walk to get to the shelter. The city was empty. Offices and shops were closed. Not many people around, no mothers and children and aunties and uncles and grandparents milling about visiting each other. Perhaps they were all walking around outside the White House, trying to get a glimpse of the President. Or they might have been down at the Mall, looking at all the monuments, trying to remember how great America was, and if that is what they were doing, it would probably have cheered them up a little.

I have been down at the Mall sometimes, as Mom's work is very close to the White House, and to all the monuments. The babysitters take me there now and then.

I asked Garrick if he ever visited the Vietnam Memorial. He said no.

I went there once, and it really wasn't a cheery memorial,

come to think about it. All those names. A sea of dead people. I remember I started crying as soon as I stepped close to the wall, even before I saw that it had all those names on it. It was like being in a fog, breathing with sadness all around it, and when I saw all those names, the whole wall came to life, with the faces and arms and legs and hearts crying, and I could hear the voices of the wives and the children and the mothers and the fathers and the friends who had visited.

The broad, straight-lined streets were empty. The sleek buildings seemed cold and dark. Some of them looked like they were made of dark mirrors. I shuddered thinking that our reflections might be zapped and caught inside those mirrors, as if we were food for the buildings, making them grow taller and shinier. Parts of us could be stuck in those shiny, dark surfaces forever.

We turned a corner and came to a street with lots of people. They looked like homeless people. Some were sitting very still on benches in the squares and parks, with their thick, gray, woolen blankets and tattered bags. They were trying to keep warm. Others sat near metro entrances, begging for money.

I know it sounds bad when I say those people looked like homeless. What I mean with that is people who hang out on corners, sit on benches, lean up to buildings. Come to think about it, perhaps their reflections have been gobbled up by the dark mirrors, without them noticing it, and they are glued to the glass surfaces, waiting for the images they once had of themselves to be released. And in that waiting, they lost their homes, someone else stole their homes, and they cannot go back there.

It was as if the streets in this city were asking me to walk fast, head first, and to keep running, to avoid getting gobbled up, or losing my home. I turned my head to look at the buildings, and all I saw was my own reflection, every ruffled hair and scruffy garment. A jacket, too small for me. My face, not beautiful at all.

"You don't really see people who have homes around here

very much," I said to Garrick. He looked at me with a strange expression, said nothing.

I will explain to you what I mean, as Garrick didn't seem interested. On weekends, most people with homes rush through the streets. It is as if they are scared of getting their reflections stolen if they slow down. Or maybe they are terrified of finding faults with their appearances. They are either running to their safe offices, or to the metro, so that they can go home to their places with fewer dark mirrors, outside the city. It's not like other places I've visited, say Italy, where people of all sorts always mill around; people with and without homes, sitting, standing, even lying on the streets. You know, when we visited Siena in Italy three years ago, there was a place shaped like a circle in the middle of the city, called Campo de Fiori. It used to be for horse racing, but when we got there it was just a lovely, empty circle, surrounded by cafes. And there were lots of people lying on the ground, inside the circle. All kinds of people who didn't look like they would normally lie on the street, just felt like sitting or lying down inside the Campo. I found it so strange. But there was something about that place, like it was inviting us to do just that, to stop rushing, and to sit or lie down, and we did. I think because it was so beautiful. The houses and the churches and the statues didn't steal my reflection, or threaten to make me homeless, but made me feel like I could also be beautiful, as if beauty belonged to me, and I belonged to it. It was because it touched that soft spot inside that I told you about, the one that when it gets going makes you forget about everything that is not important, and has you remember that you're a human being. Even Mom lay down on the street that day. From there, we enjoyed the blue sky, the ancient stone buildings and the feeling of the place. I was very surprised that Mom lay down, but she did. I could feel her so close to me, and I remember the reflection of the evening sun and a tower in her sunglasses as she turned to look at me, and all the beauty and light went inside me, and it felt like eating delicious food that would stay inside me forever.

"We're almost there," Garrick said.

We stopped in front of a building with a group of people standing and sitting outside. There were maybe fifteen people and most of them smiled and greeted Garrick when they saw him. "Hi, Gar," a man said, "don't often see you out in daylight!"

Garrick smiled and said, "See? I'm no vampire!"

Then we went inside and Garrick introduced me to Tony, the colleague who had been covering for him. Tony was a large, smiley, Afro-American guy wearing a red T-shirt with a snarling black wolf printed on the chest.

"Meet my friend Luna," Garrick said. "She is here to help out today."

We shook hands and I said, "Nice to meet you."

There was a strange smell in the building. I felt it as soon as we entered.

I asked Garrick about it and he said without smiling, "It is the smell of life on the streets. You and I take a warm shower and have clean clothes every day. It's not the case for everyone. Now, let's have a walk around and see who's here today."

We went to a large room that had computers at one end, and sofas, tables and chairs at the other. There were people everywhere. Garrick walked around and talked to some who he seemed to know. There were other workers as well, and they all wore badges. I could see their names. "Breakfast is finished in the dining hall," Garrick said, "and now there's mass. A minister offers a Sunday service at 10am. Some people are waiting for that."

One lady sitting in a chair with an open blue sports bag next to her, smiled at me. She had shiny eyes, and very wrinkly skin. Some of her front teeth were missing. She beckoned me with a claw-like hand, and I hesitantly walked towards her. "I didn't know there were any children around, Gar," she said. "Who are you young lady?"

She put her hand on my arm and looked at me intently. She was still smiling. There was a strong smell coming from her. Kind of sweet, and earthy, and bitter. It went right deep inside my nose and it spoke to me about being human in an animal body. I shivered and I wanted to run away. The smell was telling my body about dark asphalt, about urine, about blood and tears, about loneliness, and about something else that I could not grasp. I raised my head and gazed into the eyes of the lady and saw what this "something else" was about: a wild, beautiful and terrifying open landscape. I felt myself being pulled, falling into her eyes, but then I heard Garrick say, "How are you today, Betha? You've met my friend Luna, I see. We are neighbors, and we both like trees."

This pulled me back, and I managed to say to Betha that I was hanging out with Garrick because my Mom was in the hospital. Betha looked at me with her intense eyes, took my hand and said, "With Gar you are in good hands, he is a rock. That's what his name means, you know, Garrick, the rock. Back in Ireland we would know a good Garrick when we saw one. I'm Beth. That means life, so it's a good omen for your mom that we met today, girl. You can tell your mom you met Life today, and that all will be well."

I looked at her brown hands and dirty finger nails. I so wanted her to be right.

"Thank you, Betha," I managed to say.

And then Garrick said, "Come on, Luna, time to get towels and soaps. People are waiting."

We put the towels on a trolley and pushed it into a huge room. There were bunk beds, but also single beds. I stopped and looked at this room full of empty beds. There were three women and two men making beds and mopping the floor. They worked very fast. The bunk bed nearest to me had a teddy resting on a blue pillow. It looked like it had been hugged a lot. It had a kind of worn, stubby fur like my own teddy, "Piggy," from years of cuddling.

Garrick stopped and looked at me. I walked up to the bed and touched the worn teddy. "That bear belongs to Blue," he said. "I didn't think he would still be here. His mom is getting them into better housing. But it takes time."

"Where is Blue now?" I asked.

"Downstairs, maybe."

We put clean towels on top of the pillows. There were about thirty beds in rows. "There are twice as many in the Men's room," Garrick said.

I tried to imagine sleeping in here. Together with all the people downstairs. Some of whom I heard talking to themselves. I wondered if they still did that at night. "Do people get earplugs?" I asked Garrick. He shook his head.

The room felt tired. As if the bodies that slept there could never really relax and enter that restful soft, floaty place of sleep. I know how hard it is to sleep in a new place. Like having tentacles growing out of my spine and my head, reaching into the place. Sometimes I try to pull the tentacles in, because it is exhausting to feel things. Especially the things that Mom doesn't believe to be real. I used to tell her that our body is the antenna of our soul, but I stopped because she just shook her head and wondered where I got such strange ideas from. I don't know where I get my ideas from, but I think some of them are true.

Blue

Same day, 2007

We went back downstairs and walked over to the area with the sofas and tables. In a corner there was a green mat with scattered Legos, two toy cars and a boy. I saw his back in the midst of the Legos, bending over a construction. Garrick kneeled and said, "Hi, Blue, how are you today?"

The boy turned around, smiled when he saw Garrick. "Gar, build with me," he said. Garrick picked up a few Lego blocks, started putting them together. Blue turned towards me, and two bright, shiny eyes burrowed into me. He had a blue Band-Aid with a red car from the movie *Cars* on his left cheek.

"Who is girl?" he asked, pointing to me. Garrick said I was his friend Luna. He told Blue that I saw his teddy upstairs on the bed, and wanted to meet him. He smiled at me and gave me a silver car the size of my hand. "Race me," he said and picked up a green car. I bent down and put the silver car on the floor, testing its wheels. He did the same. "Ready, steady, go!" he shouted and sent the green car across the floor. It flew through the room, smashed into a man's foot. The owner of the foot turned and looked for the source of the assault. Blue laughed. The man looked annoyed and kicked it under an armchair. "No, not hurt car! My car!" Blue shouted. I walked over to the armchair and moved it a bit so I could pick up the toy. Blue came towards me, holding his hand out. I gave the car to him and he smiled. We went back to the mat where Garrick was now sitting.

"Luna, can you stay with Blue while I pop into the office and do emails?" he asked. I nodded, and picked up some Legos. "Where is your mom?" Garrick asked Blue.

He shrugged and gave me a handful of Lego blocks. "Now you make something!" Blue told me.

Garrick left, and I felt lost. Smaller kids are strange. My tummy was not right because of the smell. Blue was sneezing all over me. There was yellow, thick snot running from his nose.

I looked around for a tissue, but no one paid any attention to us. I ran to the bathroom and pulled off some toilet paper. When I got back, Blue had already wiped the snot with his sleeve, and some was smeared across his cheeks. I asked if I could wipe his face, and he gave me a skeptical look. He had stopped what he was doing, and stared at me. I wiped his nose and his cheeks, and heard myself saying, "There you are, little one, that's better! You are so cute," in a voice that wasn't quite my own. He was still staring at me, and I realized I was talking to him the same way that I used to talk to Ariel, Sigrid's dog.

We sat next to each other and built a Lego town with square houses, two toy cars and a Lego woman walking a dog. I made up that the green carpet was grass, with lots of parks and gardens for our town. He liked that. "And this is the sea," he said, pointing to the gray linoleum floor. He placed a Lego construction in the sea. "Battleship full of baddies coming to town. We fight!" he said, and started throwing the Legos in a manic way. We fought the baddies, who looked just like the goodies, and we got so mixed up about the baddies and the goodies that we tore the whole town down. Blue said, "Aliens. All blown up, nowhere to hide!"

I told him to calm down. "Let's go and find Garrick. Maybe he can find us a snack," I said.

Garrick was in the office.

Blue shouted, "Gar! Girl is good at Lego. Snack?"

Garrick turned around and smiled. "I'm glad you two had fun. There are Oreos on the table. Tony left them. You can share."

We devoured the Oreos and Blue said, "Girl stay here!" He took my hand.

"My name is Luna," I reminded him. "I can't stay here. I have a home, and my mom is in hospital. I'm going to visit her soon."

"My grandma is sick. But not in hospital," said Blue. "But when she is good, we go back, if she is still there," he added.

I sat down in an armchair in a corner of the office. There was a small TV on a table. Blue jumped onto my lap and said, "Watch with me!" I flicked through the channels and found Doc McStuffins on one of the networks. Blue's little body felt warm on top of mine. I didn't pay much attention to the cartoon. "I want to be doctor when I big," said Blue. "Then help Grandma."

It was like having a cat on my lap, and I stroked Blue's back as if I were stroking his fur. It felt good. I wanted to protect him. I sniffed him. He had a salty, sweet kind of smell. Like a warm fall day in the park, with puddles and leaves on the ground, and a warm breeze mixed with a sharp edge that told you that summer was over.

And then it was time to go and see Mom. Garrick called a cab, and told the driver to take me to the hospital. He handed me money for the ride and a piece of paper with the number of the office written on it. He said to call the office if I needed anything. He said he would come and pick me up in the hospital when his shift was over, and that we could go back home together.

I sat in the taxi cab looking out of the window. I had that feeling I recognized from being between things. The same in-between feeling.

Then the cab stopped and the driver said we were at the hospital, and I went out but I didn't recognize the place. The cab left and I was staring at the building and wondered if I was at the wrong hospital. I saw a lady who looked like she was going to visit someone, because she was carrying flowers, and I followed her, and as we turned the corner, I realized I was in the right place, it was just that the cab had left me in a spot I hadn't been before, and I didn't recognize the building, but now my feet knew the way. I went in and smiled at the woman in the reception, and told her where I was going. She said I could go ahead.

I was in the elevator where I had been with Garrick, and I remembered his blue eyes. I tried to remember the warm feeling of Blue's body on my lap, because by now I felt so cold that I was shivering. I was stuck, hanging up there, in mid-air, between, and it was cold up there.

I was standing outside Mom's room and I could feel my heart beating very fast and hard. My throat felt funny, as if someone were tying a tight knot around it to keep my heart stuffed down in my chest and not come out through my mouth.

I opened the door, and there was a smell of stale sleep, and I thought it was not very good of the nurses to keep the windows closed for Mom. Fresh air is important. We bring fresh flowers and fruit to the sick people, but mostly we should give them fresh air to breathe, I thought. I wished I could take Mom to the seaside, because the air was always fresher there, and that would be good for her. Now my feet had taken me to her bedside, and I looked at her closed eyes, and I wanted to touch her, but instead I walked over to the window and looked outside. I wanted to let in the smell of the outside world, but the window was impossible to open. How strange, to have windows that could not be opened, and to have sick people breathe sick air.

It was gray everywhere. Gray asphalt, gray buildings, gray pigeons, gray day. I started to feel gray like the wall outside. I was sure I was turning to stone as I got back to Mom's bed. I sat on the chair next to her. The stitching of my throat was really tight, and my heart had turned to stone. I could not touch Mom. My hands were lifeless in my lap. They were not my hands any more, but belonged to an old, old lady. An old lady who had lived a long life, had many children, and even cows that she milked, but now her hands were so tired and lifeless after her long life of holding and reaching and mending and carrying, that her hands refused to do anything other than nest in her lap like two very old cats, concerned only with sleeping.

Then Mom opened her eyes, but she was not inside her eyes,

if you know what I mean, like she was somewhere very far away, and her eyes were empty, and I wondered where she was. Then her eyes landed on me, and I could feel that the weight of my stone body was pulling her back into her eyes. She was so light, nothing holding her down, a feather, like her body was not there. Her eyes stuck to my stone body, which was a good thing, because the rock in me was like a magnet, pulling her back into her own body, and she started coming through her eyes. I still couldn't move. I had to sit there quietly, letting the magnetic force, the love between my rock body and Mom's runaway soul do its job.

And then she was there, and she smiled, and I could feel that there was weight in her body again, and at that very moment, my body turned back to normal, and my hands were my own hands, and I reached out to touch Mom's hand at exactly the same time as she reached out to grab mine, and I climbed up on the bed and lay down beside her, and although she smelt of stale hospital air, she also smelt like Mom. The best smell in the world. I put my head against her chest and smelt her breasts. Since I was little, I could always tell how Mom was doing by smelling her breasts. They did not smell their best selves, but they smelt like home.

Tree Talk

Washington, D.C., Late Monday evening after Thanksgiving, 2007

We were sitting on Garrick's big red sofa.

I was looking out of the window, seeing the dark shape of my Oak leaning over into Garrick's yard, one big branch very close to his window.

"Are you ever worried that the wind will break off a branch from our tree and crush your house," I asked.

"No," said Garrick. "Are you?"

"No," I said. "But Mom is."

"Well, she could have told me. She still can," he answered.

I stayed quiet.

"You know that trees talk to each other, all the time, and help each other?" Garrick said.

I looked up. It was dark outside. My throat was still sown up from the visit to the hospital. I felt homeless. "Yes, trees talk to each other. They send nutrients and chemicals through underground networks," Garrick continued. "Networks of fungi and roots working together."

I understood that he was trying to distract me, make me think of something other than Mom, so I showed him that I was listening: "I was sure trees and plants talked to each other through their fragrances," I said.

He told me that trees have a very intelligent way of helping each other, and that fungi play a big part in this. The fungi exchange the minerals they get from the soil for the sugars the trees produce. In difficult times, the trees use these underground systems to send warning signals, alerting neighbors to build up defenses against pests, diseases or draughts. Resourceful trees look out for less fortunate ones. Resourceful trees share carbon and other nutrients with hungry trees. "You don't see many homeless, redundant trees in the forest," he said smiling. (My summer tutor, Mr. Evans, would be very happy about this conversation around trees. Perhaps I will write him a letter as well.)

This is what Garrick told me, "During the summer, the Paper Birches at the edge of our land in Ireland sent food to the Douglas-firs a bit further down. The Douglas-firs got overshadowed by leafier trees, and needed a bit of help from the Birches. Then in the fall, the Douglas-firs returned the favor by sending carbon back the other way."

Resource sharing happened all over the forest, he told me. With some older trees helping seedlings just starting off in life. He pointed to a magazine with an article about this. I was welcome to borrow it if I wanted. He said that when loggers cut a forest clear, or when climate change disturbs an eco-system, parts of those networks go silent. If a tree falls in a forest and its communication lines are down, no other tree would hear it fall.

"Your mom still has some healthy roots... through you. You came to talk to me when you needed help, didn't you? And you knew I was a tree. A walking tree." He smiled.

I looked at him feeling the stitch in my throat soften and my heart coming up into my mouth. I said I needed to rest and went to my bedroom so I could let my heart come out and write you.

I wonder what type of tree this notebook once was. It is hard to believe that the white paper grew out of the dark soil.

My words are like insects living in a mighty tree.

Blue is a little tree. I wonder if he has fallen asleep in that big hall full of beds and trees that nobody will hear if they fall.

The Talent Show

Washington, D.C., USA, the Tuesday after Thanksgiving, 2007

The next day I decided to go to school. It seemed like Mom was resting on dry land, and I thought going to school would make everything normal again. I got my books and my bag from our house. I took the school bus. Everything felt the same. And everything felt different.

I sat in class, heard the teachers' voices, watched myself put my arm up, answer questions, while I was really somewhere else. How did I do that? Think, answer questions, write, without really being there? It was like a ghost was doing it all for me, and I was watching this ghostly presence play my part.

Mom needed to stay in hospital for the week. Uncle Jakob called to tell me he would be with me in a week's time. But that was when Mom would be back, I told him. It didn't make any sense. But he insisted that he would be coming. I stayed on at Garrick's, of course.

Wednesday night was the school's talent show. People had been practicing for weeks. I had never participated in any talent show. Wasn't quite sure I had talents, or at least any talent others would enjoy seeing on a stage.

I asked Garrick if he wanted to come. My friend Geraldine was going to sing.

Garrick had changed his work schedule and was free at nights. He wanted to come.

We rode the bus to school. There was a crowd outside the auditorium. I hesitated. Everyone was excited, and most people had dressed up in glitter and bright colors. I was wearing a black hoodie and my old tattered jeans.

I guess we stood out from the crowd, me all gloomy, and

Garrick with his long white beard and black clothes. We looked like characters from a fantasy novel.

The doors opened. We found two seats in the back.

We didn't talk, just sat there. There was a warm feeling in the auditorium, sparkly and friendly.

The principal welcomed everyone, said something about talent taking so many forms, and that she always tried to support people finding theirs.

Then there was a big cheer, and the curtains went up. Two boys from my class, Thomas and Bertie were toastmasters. They had dressed up like adults, with suits and bow ties, and were talking like game-show hosts. I looked at Garrick to see if he got any of the fast-paced, rehearsed jokes they were warming the audience up with. He smiled at me.

Then there was a string of talents entering the stage. A girl skipped rope while bouncing on a pogo stick, moving in time with Beyonce's music. A boy did amazing yo-yo tricks, while his sister sang *Big Girls Don't Cry*. Four guys had made a "Gangsta Rap" with words of Dr Seuss's *Green Eggs and Ham*. They were dressed to look the part, and the crowd went wild, cheering and whistling. Three girls danced to Justin Timberlake's *What Goes Around, Comes Around*. And then came ballet girls and karate boys, magicians and the boy from grade eight, who all the girls in my class had a crush on, playing the guitar, singing John Mayer's *In Your Atmosphere*. It was beautiful. Five girls dressed in net stockings and red silk dresses with short tutus, danced to Rihanna's *Shut Up and Drive*. One boy played the violin while everyone chatted and made distracting noises.

Then Geraldine was there.

She walked out on the stage in a short dress with a print of the American flag all over it. She had a bow in her hair with stars and stripes, red tights, and cowboy boots. Her face looked white, and her lips were very red from the new lipstick she had showed me last time I went to her house.

I realized I hadn't talked to her in a while, so I didn't know what she would be performing. Perhaps I was not such a good friend. Maybe she had told me about it, but I couldn't remember.

I turned to Garrick and whispered, "That's Geraldine, my friend."

Then the music started.

She sang in a monotone voice, and her face was like a blank mask. As if she were empty. I saw my friend up there on the stage, but what I heard was not quite her. It was as if something had borrowed her body to sing through her:

They arrive with empty eyes
Without a name or face
Mothers, children, fathers, too
A dream, a nightmare, to a place.
No space for you
No room at all
Carry children on their backs
No one to catch you when you fall.
Caravan to the Land of Plenty
Caravan to the Land of Plenty
Caravan to the Land of Plenty

What? I had never heard this song. Never even heard Geraldine sing it. Country, seriously ?!? Not our style at all. Music this lame! Did her dad, or her mom play this song at home?

Give us your sweat and toil
No bread to eat
One fish to fill a crowd
No shoes on our feet.
We are the herd, the many
Reaching for a hand
Where is the love to share

Here in the Promised Land
Caravan to the Land of Plenty
Caravan to the Land of Plenty
Caravan to the Land of Plenty

I looked at her up on the stage, all wrapped in the American flag, and she felt so different from me. I did not understand why she seemed so different.

Across the desert path
The road is worn and long
Then dust gets in our eyes
We walk on without a song
Caravan to the Land of Plenty
Caravan to the Land of Plenty
Caravan to the Land of Plenty

I imagined Sigrid wrapped in the Norwegian flag. What song would she be singing?

I could never wear the American flag, nor the Norwegian. Then I remembered that Mom told Uncle Jakob that if he didn't sign the papers, I would become the property of America, which would make Geraldine's flag my flag too. But I don't think I would ever wear a flag.

But Geraldine could wear the American flag. Or the flag could wear Geraldine. They were a perfect match somehow… America was singing through her... without her having the faintest idea about it. At least that was what it seemed to me.

I sat up straight as the whole auditorium fell silent.

Geraldine's body was transparent, it had become a window, and we could see something through her. It was like being in a car with her, looking out of the window, onto the promised land. Driving with Geraldine, without a goal, through the desert and the endless highways. We could see the Grand Canyon, the shopping malls, the guns, the trailer homes, the hopes and dreams, the shootings in churches and schools, Death Valley, the holiday parades and the Halloween houses. We passed Disneyland, a golden tower, the Native Americans and their casinos, military babies and mothers and fathers in uniforms. We kept driving through the desert, and there was George W. Bush, and there was Mom, and the cheerleaders in short skirts, and guys bashing each other on football fields, and police waving guns, and black people running, and there was the Statue of Liberty and hamburgers, and homeless people scattered on the streets, and people landing on the moon, and Hollywood stars in beautiful dresses, and the Golden Gate Bridge, and we were in the desert again, and Geraldine gave us water. And we drank it. Geraldine sang the desert beautiful, sang it into spring time, and it was blooming, and I have no idea how she did it. Her red lips were moving, her eyes half closed, and there was a beep in my ear.

Across the desert path
The road is worn and long
Then dust gets in our eyes
And we walk on without a song
Carry children on our backs
No one to catch you when you fall
Caravan to the Land of Plenty
Caravan to the Land of Plenty
Caravan to the Land of Plenty

There was a moment of silence when Geraldine's song ended. She seemed confused. She was looking out at us with her own eyes again. Then everyone cheered. The moment of confusion was gone, and Geraldine smiled and waved at us like a real star.

Garrick took my hand and whispered in my ear, "She is really good your friend... Really good!"

Tomato and Cheese at Night

Washington, D.C., USA November, same night as the talent show 2007

Back home and there was a flashing light on Garrick's answering machine.

A voice from the hospital: "Please call back at this number. It is urgent."

I watched him pick up the receiver, dial the number. His face was gray.

He waited a long time before anyone picked up on the other end.

He told them his name and mentioned Mom.

Then he said, "Yes, OK, I understand. Yes. Yes, in the morning."

He hung up, and I looked at him without breathing.

He took my hand and led me towards the sofa.

We sat down next to each other.

He said, "She is getting worse. They want us to go and see her first thing in the morning."

I nodded. Turned to look out of the window. It was dark. The street lights couldn't brighten up the night.

I said I wanted to go over to my house and have a bath. Asked if Garrick could come with me and wait downstairs. He could read or watch TV I told him. He nodded.

We went over together. It felt like we had just landed on the moon, gravity was not working, and we were walking in big moon suits.

I went upstairs, filled the bath. The sound of the water was soothing and familiar. I put some of Mom's bath foam in. I wanted to smell her.

I lay in the scolding hot bath. It was burning. I could not think when the heat burned my skin. I didn't want to. But then I got used to it, and the thoughts rushed back in.

I was picturing you. It would have been a good moment for you to turn up.

But I know that you will not.

Ever.

Turn up.

I got out of the bath, picked up clean clothes. A green sweater and black jeans.

Went downstairs to find Garrick reading my book about light.

He put it down when he saw me.

I asked, "Do you have a driver's license?"

"Yes," he said, "but I don't have car."

"Can we go for a drive? I know where Mom's car keys are."

He looked at me intently, trying to understand what was going on in my mind.

"Where would you like to go?"

"Just go for a drive," I repeated. "Please."

He took a deep breath.

"OK, let's go."

The car keys were hanging on a nail beside the front door. I grabbed them and gave them to Garrick.

We walked out in silence.

He opened the car and I sat in the front. He didn't say anything.

"Where to?" he asked as he turned the key.

"Just drive," I said. "To the desert, to the Land of Plenty."

Garrick smiled.

"There are no deserts around here. Urban sprawl... kind of a desert. And then fields with trees and farms. Choose Maryland or Virginia," he said. "I guess it doesn't make much difference. Both states carry the name of the Holy Mother. Mary and the Virgin..."

We drove down our block.

"Maryland," I said.

Garrick turned right.

I tried to turn on the radio. Mom always listened to NPR. They didn't play much music, only non-stop talking about the world.

I wanted music.

"How do I find a music station?"

He fiddled with the dials and suddenly there was music.

"This kind of thing?" he asked.

"I guess so. Is it American music?" I wanted to feel the same bittersweet despair and hope that I had felt when Geraldine sang that old song.

"Definitely. This is folk music," he said.

I looked out of the window. We drove through a main street. No one was outside.

I turned the volume up and sank into the car seat.

Garrick didn't speak.

We drove through suburb after suburb. I looked at the lights in the houses. They seemed warm and cozy in the cold dark night. This was where people rushed to during the rush hour. To their warm and snug homes. My home felt cold and dark.

The music changed to rap. I didn't mind. Garrick said it was still American.

We stopped at a service station and Garrick pumped gas. When he was done he asked if I was hungry.

I was.

There was a Subway and we bought sandwiches. I found it hard to focus on the fillings, so I just said, "Cheese and tomato."

We sat down at a corner table. It was gray and dirty. There were orange plastic chairs all around. The floor was brown. The lights white and cold. Everything looked unreal.

We ate in silence.

Then Garrick said, "We can see the stars when we get a bit further out."

We got back into the car.

Down a smaller road, I saw trees outside the windows. And fields. And farms.

We were the only people out in the night.

He pulled off the road and stopped the car, went outside, came around and opened my door.

The night smelled of damp soil, trees, and of winter.

Garrick leaned his back against the car… I did the same.

Stars. Far away. I gazed at them. I felt very small.

I moved closer to Garrick.

"In the city the lights are so bright, it's hard to see. Here it's easier," he said.

We gazed up at the sky. Side by side.

"Will she be OK?" I asked

"I don't know," he answered.

Silence. For a long time. Then he said, "But you will. You will be OK. Regardless."

He looked at me very seriously. Then he looked back up at the sky.

We stood there for a while longer.

I could feel my feet on the ground. The smells were vivid and fresh. So vivid that it was like drinking the trees and the soil with my nose.

The contours of the trees were gleaming, the light from the moon strong enough to cover the dark forest in a silver coat. We had parked near an opening in the thick forest. I glimpsed a path going into the dark. Something rustled, and a bird flew up.

I saw clearly in the night. I smelled the trees. I could hear the silence. I felt the cold air, and the warmth from Garrick's body. My eyes were my eyes, my body my body. I was not hanging in the air. Gravity was working. I was not wearing a moon-suit. I was not swim-flying. There was no beep alerting me of anything. I was simply me.

I didn't know whether Mom would live or die.

But somehow I knew that Garrick was right. I would be OK.

Just as that sank in, Garrick looked at me. "That's right. You got it. Do you want to go home now?"

I nodded.

We drove the long way home. Without music this time. Just the engine and the wheels on the road.

We didn't talk.

Garrick said we could still have a couple of hours' sleep before we went to see Mom.

He said he would wake me up when it was time.

Light

Washington, D.C., USA, the Thursday after Thanksgiving, 2007

He woke me up. I got dressed, ate porridge. We rode the bus, then the metro, and then we walked the last bit to the hospital.

Garrick talked to the receptionist.

We took the elevator, walked down the corridor.

Garrick opened the door, gestured for me to walk in.

There was no air in the room, so I took a deep breath.

Garrick came in behind me and stood by the door.

There was a nurse in the room. She smiled at me.

I walked towards Mom's bed.

She was sleeping. There was a mask covering her mouth and nose. It was connected to a beeping machine.

I wanted her to open her eyes. I needed to see if this machine had taken all the life out of her, made her into a machine, too. I hadn't been able to do my work on her, keeping her alive and human lately. She had spent too much time in this room without air, and with all those machines around her.

The nurse said she might not become conscious.

She pushed a chair close to the bed, so I could sit next to her.

I took Mom's hand.

The nurse removed the mask from her face. "She can have a break now," she said.

I was trying to think whether I had seen any movies where a child had to sit by the mother's bed in hospital. I could not think of any. If I had seen a movie about it, I would have known a little more of what to do. A child was not supposed to be in a situation like that. A mother was supposed to look after the child, not the other way around.

I felt angry, but I couldn't be, as it would not be very nice to be angry if Mom woke up.

Then I took her hand, felt her skin. It was silky soft, in a mushy kind of way.

I thought that if I squeezed her hand hard, she might open her eyes, and then I would do a funny face, tell her a joke or read her one of my poems, and she would snap out of this lifeless thing she seemed to be stuck in.

I squeezed her hand gently, and she did open her eyes. She looked my way, but didn't see me. The machine had finally won, turned her into a thing.

I squeezed her hand again.

Her eyes were trying to land on me. And they did. She landed, and she saw me.

I tried to smile, but something in me knew that this was different from all the other times. I felt it deep in my tummy, or in my heart, or in the place where all this kind of knowing happens. It was different.

"I was waiting for you," she said in a faint voice. "You will be OK," she said.

"I know," I whispered.

"Just always be you," she said. She tried to smile.

"Promise me that. Never forget to be you, because there is no one else like you in the world. And it would be so sad if everyone became like everyone else, right?"

I could not speak. I was part of her.

"I will always be with you, Luna, you know that, right?"

"Yes, I know," I said.

I pulled my chair even closer to her. "Can I climb up next to you?" I asked.

She tried to make space for me, but she couldn't move.

I squeezed as gently as I could into the bed next to her.

"You smell of peaches," she strained to say.

I closed my eyes. Her body felt so weak. I knew that she was about to leave.

I tried to make my body heavy, tried to call her back, but she was floating, and I ended up with her in the dark sea. It was soft and dark, velvety soft. Like how I imagined it must have felt when being in her tummy before I was born. Soft and inside. In the water. But this inside also felt like it had no end or outside, as if it expanded into foreverness. I could feel me, and I could feel Mom there. We were two, and at the same time we were absolutely, completely one.

"My daughter," she whispered in my ear.

I whispered back, "I love you, Mom."

Then the dark became a bright glimmer, and then there was only light. It was in me and around me. It was coming from everywhere and nowhere. It went into my body, and it came from my body. It came from Mom's body, and it came from outside of Mom's body.

Everything was completely open, and bright.

Then her body became limp, and the room was fully alight. Like there was sunrise, or a sunset happening right there in the room.

I stayed in the light for a long time, or a short time, I don't know, because there was no time in that light. All I knew was that I needed to stay in that light and to help Mom to wherever she was going.

I knew she needed my help and I did what I could.

I had to help her keep the space open and the light bright.

I felt her moving out, slowly. I felt all the love that was in her move into my body, and I felt the light that had belonged to her body go into me. The light that was in her spirit was leaving, but the light of her body went into me. I had wondered about that. Ever since I heard about the dead fireflies light up the skin of those boys.

Now I knew.

And then the room changed. The light faded, and it faded even more, and I knew she was gone.

I sat up. Looked towards the nurse and Garrick, and they came over. The nurse did whatever a nurse does when someone dies.

A doctor came in and did something too.

Garrick took my hand, sat me down on a chair in the opposite corner of the room.

Mom had gone.

She had left.

The body in the bed was just empty now.

Mom was not in here anymore.

I'm not ready to be my own mom... and dad.

I am only twelve years old.

PART II

The Parcel II

Tromsø, Norway, November 2018

These letters were written for you, and never sent.

Now the words are here. They fill my white desk and crowd my head as I look out of the window. Just like I used to do in D.C., watching Garrick walk slowly in his yard back then. Now I watch the snow melt instead. Black snow. It was pure and soft and now it is hard, dirty and icy.

When Mom died I stopped writing.

At the beginning I thought the layers of snow around my heart would never budge. The ice was too thick. No thawing possible. No words would flow onto the page. My hands were numb and cold, like wet toads, hopping, without direction. I closed my body. My chest caved in. I found it hard to stand up straight.

I'm twenty-two now.

These pages are the first I have written not required by a teacher since I was twelve.

I am not writing to you anymore.

Now I write for my own life.

I think I always did.

I don't know if my soul is still OK. My body is not. It feels crooked and dried up. I keep on trying to straighten it out, find a better posture. My muscles twist around my skeleton, lock me in. My hands are always cold and damp. When I touch someone, I can feel them flinch, see them pull back from my wet, toad-like hands. Even dogs do this.

My arms hang like frozen wings.

I don't think God ever liked the look of my face.

I moved back to Jakob's house in Norway when I was twelve.

I still live there. I know I should have moved out a long time ago, but I never found a good reason for leaving. He is never here, and the cleaner who comes every week doesn't interfere with anything I do. I tutor kids while I try to get into medical school. If I can't get in this year, I'll have to think of something else. I see Sigrid most weeks. She will be moving to Oslo in the spring. Law school.

I have done what was expected of me. Always did my homework, learned to play the piano, went skiing in the winter, traveled with friends in Europe the summer I turned eighteen, got drunk, had boyfriends.

But my soul could not straighten out my twisted body and my wet, toad-like hands.

Every week, since I was twelve, I spoke to Garrick on the phone at night.

He talked to me about the changes happening in the U.S., about Obama, the war in Afghanistan, government shut downs, the Affordable Care Act, and the Dalai Lama at the White House. He talked to me about Trump, about walls, immigration and gun laws. About women taking to the streets. He told me stories about people in the shelter. About the Oak in my old backyard. He kept talking when I could not. He kept talking to keep me alive, told stories for me to remember, when all I wanted was to forget.

Still, I kept calling him back.

I almost went to visit him once, but then I didn't. I couldn't face the thought of seeing our old house.

I wanted him to come and visit me, but he said he didn't do well with long journeys any more. Maybe that was for the best. I don't believe Sigrid or Jakob would have understood about Garrick and me.

Three months ago, I received the parcel through the mail.

A letter announced that Garrick had died.

It was from Jennifer, the other neighbor. Garrick had made her promise to mail me the package when he was gone.

Garrick, the song I found in the Oak, which I kept finding in his heart from the beginning to the very end.

I think about the arrows we all send out, arrows of desire... for contact, for love, for meaning. I understand now that we cannot control who finds them. Mine had not been shot far. It got caught in the top of our Oak outside my window. Garrick picked it up. What a strange design there is behind seemingly random incidents!

What part of us shoots arrows out into the world, and who rides on them?

What brings someone towards an arrow?

What makes them know that that arrow is just for them?

And who sings the song that secretly resides in the center of all things?

My arrows were broken a long time ago. I have not shot any since the one that landed in the Oak.

There was a letter from Garrick in the parcel, in his usual style:

Dear Luna,

When you read this, I will have left this life-world.

I am sitting in my living room, in my usual armchair. It is dark outside, so the lamp is lit. As I write, uncomfortably hunched over a magazine with Putin on the cover, I feel the great Silence moving closer. It is pulling me into itself, or I'm pulling it into me. It erases everything as I become it... it feels like falling... or joining gravity... or being pulled into the magnetic force that holds it all in place... falling, like a snowflake. It's terrifying and amazing, the force that creates and erases everything. It has weight, but not a weight that can be measured. It is absolute weight, and absolute weightlessness at once.

I look outside the window from this place of weightless weight, and everything belongs. It is all perfect. Your Oak, the first bridge between our two worlds, is perfect. More beautiful than I ever noticed. The branches, with a few stubborn leaves, hanging on, resisting the pull of gravity, remind me we are all different. The trunk, spontaneously rising from the ground, full and empty. The roots, all covered up, reaching down, connecting to other roots, connecting us, Luna.

I look at our Oak. Then at your small, painted dragonfly rock on my mantelpiece, and I know that some things cannot be erased. The Oak, the rock and my body will all disappear, but that which is concealed within their form will not. And what is that? What is that which cannot be erased, Luna?

I sit here in my shabby old armchair, almost completely consumed by the Silence, and I am beginning to see that nothing is really outside of this, not even death ... it's all inside, everything is, the good and the bad, the stillness and the movement, the formless and the form.

So when you find the golden, liquid light you used to talk to me about, you'll know that we are still in contact. Just not through the phone.

Love,
Garrick

I put the letter away. I put it on the top of my tallest shelf, the one that I can only reach by standing on a chair.

I did not want to remember.

Then I went back on the chair to read the letter again.

I have done this many times over the last three months.

In the parcel there was also the book I read while Mom was dying. For three months I have been looking at it without opening it. For three months I have been sifting through my old handwriting, searching for proof of survival, for color or light kept in the wings of those little dead, black, word bodies. For three months I have been dreaming of Garrick. Garrick laughing at me, night after night. Garrick dressed as a pirate, standing on the bow of a ship, pointing to a sea of dung. That sea stank. I was on that ship too, staring at that festering sea.

Then one night Garrick the pirate told me to look beyond the sea of dung. He was pointing to something near the horizon. He laughed and said, "You are a luminous fish, why sail around in shit? Jump in and swim over there!" I couldn't see what he was pointing to.

And then I heard it. Only a thought, at the beginning. A two-dimensional sound, like a word without flesh. Then it started to vibrate. A faint beep in my ear. Tinnitus, I thought. Probably what it was all the time. Tinnitus brought on by stress. It is not uncommon.

I wonder what the twelve-year-old me would see if she looked at me now?

How would she make sense of what I have become?

A butterfly, a dragonfly or a firefly?

I remember telling Mom that the body is the antenna of the soul, but when the soul is lost, or frozen, the body has neither light nor color. It becomes a rigid shell.

A cockroach.

Garrick left me his house.

Death brings me yet another empty home.

Isn't it funny how houses are being left to me?

I don't have to worry about my retirement saving anymore.

He also left me a brief note, together with open flight tickets to Greece, and for a boat trip from Athens to the Island of Hydra:

There is a white house with a red door on the street that connects the harbor with Kala Pigada, on the Greek island of Hydra. Just five minutes from the port and three houses up from the Hotel Miranda, where there is a room for you,

I'm sure you will find it!

Love,

Garrick

Thanksgiving II

Hydra, Greece, November 21, 2018

I stand on the front deck of the ferry. I have been here for almost two hours, since we left Athens. The smell of salty sea is mixed with diesel, and makes my skin and hair feel greasy.

The boat is slowing down as we approach the port of Hydra.

The blue light of the sea pierces my eyes.

I am twenty-two years old. I am wearing a black, crocheted shawl. I pull it tighter to fend off the wind.

I am cold.

It's off season, so there are not many tourists.

If this were in America, we would be celebrating Thanksgiving tomorrow.

What a cliché for my Dad to choose to live here. Mom was right. This is the perfect place for wannabe artists and searchers of miracles. All hoping to be the next Leonard Cohen. But Cohen moved on. He knew when it was time to leave, and it was a different time then. Those who stayed went nowhere. They were stranded here with the donkeys, the tourists, the refugees, and the broken dreams.

Garrick's last wish was for me to travel to this pathetic place. I am doing it for him. I am no longer searching for a father, nor for miracles. I did that when I was twelve.

The boat has docked. A few people get off.

I pick up my rucksack and walk across the landing.

White and blue fishing boats gently bop in the waves.

There are two young men waving "room for rent" signs. They approach me and reveal in their broken English that they have the "perfect place" for me. One grabs my arm. I shake my head and say, "I don't need anything."

They don't believe me and do their best to lure me into a

guided tour. "Today? Tomorrow? Car? Motorcycle? Very good!"

I say, "No," and make my way towards a group of fishermen further along.

I ask if someone can point me in the direction of the Hotel Miranda, Kala Pigadia. An old man shows me the way.

I walk the narrow road. I see no donkeys, but signs in Greek and English advertising natural springs. I have read that Hydra means water in Greek, and that the wells are still used by the locals. A pointed sign shows the way to an old mansion.

I must have walked for exactly five minutes when I find myself outside the Hotel Miranda. I stop and look back at the narrow, cobbled road behind me, white and grey stone walls. Then I step into the Hotel Miranda.

The reception is decorated with eighteenth- and nineteenth-century furniture and antiques. The ceiling is covered in what looks like Italian frescoes. I take a deep breath and wish that Garrick could have been here with me.

I say I have a reservation. The receptionist tells me that the room is already fully paid for one week. They have held the payment for a while, awaiting my reservation. I get the key and walk down the hallway and up a staircase leading to a room facing the harbor.

I open the door and enter a large white room with a yellow ceiling. There are patterns of squares and flowers in reds, blues and greens painted on the yellow vaulting. A red velvet sofa and a comfortable-looking bed, all seducing me to relax. I remove my black shawl; it does not fit the space.

There are abstract paintings on the walls. My eyes are drawn to one hanging above the bed. Dark and light blue, golden, white... looks like the sea, or the sky, or neither. The shapes coming out of the blue seem to reveal faces, springing out of the formless, sea-like landscape.

A wave surges in my chest, and I feel dizzy. I sit down on the red velvet sofa, thinking I haven't found my land legs after the boat trip.

My old, battered rucksack also looks out of place in this room. I chuck it into a large wardrobe.

I open the balcony door, and there's the sea again. The harbor, and the blue beyond. I get my water bottle from my bag and sit down on the balcony, sip mindlessly while I take in the view. Rooftops, churches, bright red bougainvillea climbing white walls. Blue sky, blue sea. And a donkey tied to a pole not far up the road.

I take a shower, leave my room and find a cafe by the harbor. I eat a Greek salad.

Then I walk back up the narrow, cobbled street. I pass the Hotel Miranda, and I walk up to where I saw the donkey standing.

There is a white house with blue windowsills, red geraniums and a red door. No donkey now, but names next to the red door.

Elpida, Dorea, Erik.

Erik.

My heart starts racing and I can't help it.

I stand there for what feels like an eternity. I am not able to go towards the door, nor to walk back the way I came. I have to accept my fate. I have looked at something which was not for my eyes, and the Gods have turned me into stone. I am hoping that I blend in with the Greek surroundings, and that passers-by will think it normal to see a female sculpted and placed outside a house.

I stand there while pigeons land beside me, peck at the hard soil, and then take off. I stand there while a stray dog walks past and sniffs my hand. I stand there until the light changes, and the afternoon sun is starting to take its leave.

I stand there until a girl, looking about eleven or twelve years old comes down the street and stops next to me. She smiles, and says something in Greek.

"Sorry," I say. "I don't speak Greek. English?"

"You wait what?" she says and smiles. Her eyes are bright. Her skin bronze.

"Do you live here?" I manage to ask, pointing to the house with the red door.

"Yes," she smiles.

"And Erik... is your dad? Father?" I stutter.

"You know Erik?" she says, and the brightness of her eyes disappear.

"No... Maybe," I say.

We look at each other in silence. Trying to understand what is going on, like animals sniffing each other out.

I am a statue, a talking statue.

"My mother is in house," she says. "You come in?"

I cannot move.

The girl walks up the few steps to the red door. She opens it and calls, "Mama, come, talk English!"

A woman, looking in her fifties, comes to the door. She has a purple jacket on, and long wavy hair, which must have been very black, but now mostly gray. She is beautiful. She looks at me. Her eyes are kind. "Can I help you?" she asks.

I swallow. I am an opossum. I am frozen, immobilized. I am hoping this dangerous woman of prey will not see me if I play dead.

She comes up to me, touches my shoulder, and asks, "Are you OK? Do you need help?"

The touch brings me back a little. I have to respond to her.

"I am fine," I whisper. "Sorry."

Then I ask, "Is Erik at home?"

Her kind eyes look down, and the same shadow I saw in the girl's eyes comes over hers.

"Who are you? Do you know him?" she asks.

"I don't know," I say. "Or, maybe... I would like to know him. Can I ask you... is Erik from Norway?"

The lady looks straight at me, trying to see something that is not visible on the surface.

"Yes," she finally answers.

"Can I meet him?" I ask.

She looks away.

"Why?" she asks.

"We might be related," I whisper.

The girl asks something in Greek. She must be wondering what is going on.

The woman beckons me in, and we enter through the red door into a hallway decorated with woven tapestries in bright colors.

I follow her into a kitchen. It is modern with a wooden table and orange painted chairs. There are flowers in a blue ceramic vase on the counter, and I can see the doorless cupboards filled with colorful cups and plates that look handmade. I am wondering if she made the pots and cups and vases. She looks like someone who can form beautiful objects out of clay.

We sit down.

She is still looking kind, but has a shadow of worry and sadness hanging over her.

"You and Erik related, you say?" she asks.

"He might be my father," I say, and l cannot meet her eyes.

She is completely still. I am not able to detect a reaction in her.

"I see," she finally says.

"Erik upstairs. Not well... A stroke to his left side. Two months ago."

I stop breathing.

"He is better now, but cannot speak. I am not sure what he understands."

I stare at her, as if I, too, have lost my language comprehension.

What she is saying does not make any sense. What she is telling me is impossible. I spent my childhood collecting words for this man, and she wants me to believe that he will not understand anything I say to him.

How perfect! I will leave with my toad hands and roach shell intact.

No one says anything for what seems to be too long a time. There are no obvious words, so we sit there with the feelings that are forming between us. Numbness, despair, disappointment, relief, grief, fear.

I am in a daze for a while.

Then I look at the young girl. She must be his daughter.

"What is your name?" I ask, wondering if she will say Elpida or Dorea.

"Dorea," she answers.

"I'm Luna."

"Elpida," says her mom.

They are losing a father and a husband. I am not losing anything.

"I'm sorry," I say. "I am sorry for you!"

Elpida stands up and says she will make tea.

Dorea is doodling on a paper left on the table.

Elpida comes back with mugs on a tray and a steaming teapot. She pours hot water into cobalt-blue ceramic cups.

She asks about me, and about my mother.

She listens. The kindness coming from this stranger touches my body. It is a physical sensation of warmth. In response, words flow out of me like liquid that has been held underground, dammed up for a long time.

She tells me she knew about my mother. Erik told stories about her. He told stories about everything... and always, she says. She knew about my family, Uncle Jakob, Granddad, Grandma... But she did not know about me, and from what she could understand, neither did Erik.

"I guess she didn't tell him. Must have had her reasons. Erik not good at keeping secrets. Believes secrets stop life." She smiles. "Also, he always wanted a child of his own. We tried for years... but no."

I look towards Dorea, and Elpida says, "Yes, Dorea is our daughter!"

I wonder what she means, but keep quiet.

Then Elpida asks if I want to meet Erik.

I do want to see him.

We walk up the white staircase. The walls are covered by paintings and prints. Elpida tells me Erik made them.

At the top of the staircase, on the facing wall, is a painting that looks familiar. I stop and look at it. "I saw this in the Hotel Miranda," I say.

"He made many versions of this," Elpida says. She explains that he kept painting the faces in the sea. "The people he rescued, and the ones he couldn't. They haunted him, and he painted them, over and over again. His work is all over Greek islands, even in Athens."

She opens a door to the left of the staircase. I follow her into the room. Dorea is behind me.

There is a big, wooden bed facing open French windows. I can see a backyard through the windows. There are light, white cotton curtains draping the windows.

I take a few steps towards the man who is propped up with big pillows. His eyes are closed. He looks tall. His hair is mostly gray, but peppered with black strands. His hands are resting on top of the duvet. Brown, rugged hands. They look like hands that have worked outside. I can see the wind and the sun in those hands, and the ghosts of tools used often. And paintbrushes, I imagine.

They look like intelligent hands. Not fleshy and dead like office hands, which never touch the elements or trust their own particular knowing.

I look down at my own hands. They are white, completely pale. All the blood has been drained from them. I try to look for a resemblance in shape or in form to his hands, but cannot see any. My hands are wet toads.

I stand lifeless next to the bed.

Elpida brings me a chair and I sit down.

I remember how my hands had felt dead in my lap next to Mom's bed in the hospital.

Although bloodless, my toad hands hop, touch the weatherbeaten, right hand of my father.

A wet, slimy frog on a warm, dry hand. The sun is living in his hand.

Erik opens his eyes. I am looking into a pair of blue eyes.

I feel presence coming into his hand, and he meets my toad hand.

He looks at me, but I cannot tell if he sees me.

"Erik, someone special is here to see you," says Elpida. "This is Luna. From Norway. Your daughter."

I notice a slight change in his hand in response to these words, like a quiver.

I try to smile at him and say,

"Erik... Du er min far... You are my father."

"Mamma... Else fortalte... Mom told me."

I'm not able to complete the sentence. I feel awkward speaking Norwegian to him, and English feels equally wrong. But when he hears me speaking Norwegian, it seems like there is a response in him. As if he were trying to sit up straight, but his body would not let him.

"Jeg er glad for endelig å treffe deg," I say.

I hold his hand in what I realize is a tight grip. The toad has turned into a reptile, a lizard.

I know that he most likely cannot understand my words, but all I can say is, "Jeg er din datter."

Elpida and Dorea leave the room to give us some space.

I sit in numbness.

I am ready to go back to Norway, and to live in my twisted body. There are no happy endings.

Then, after what feels like a very long time, the door opens and Dorea comes back. She comes up to the bed, leans over and kisses Erik on the cheek.

She runs out of the room and comes back straight away with a notebook in her hands. She pulls out a stool and sits down next to me. She looks at me and smiles, and then she starts reading in Greek. She stops to look at Erik from time to time, and after a while she falls quiet. She takes Erik's hand and tickles it, looks annoyed when there is no response. Then she kisses the hand and holds it to her cheek.

She lets go of his hand and looks at me. "Your father, too?" she says and smiles. "Me sister!" Elpida must have explained the situation to her.

Her words shock me. *Sister*. She thinks I am her sister.

She takes my right hand, the lizard, and puts her warm palm against it. She is comparing our hands. "Me little," she says and laughs as she sees how much bigger my hand is. "You big sister."

My lizard hand feels her warm puppy hand. She is a warm-blooded mammal. I am a cold-blooded reptile. She pulls her stool close to mine, and sits so that her leg touches my leg, and the side of her torso, my torso. She reaches to my shoulder.

Then Elpida comes and says we should go downstairs and eat. The nurse will arrive in a moment. She tells me I can come back and see Erik in the morning.

Back in the kitchen I feel awkward. I don't know what to do. Elpida asks me to sit down, pours me a glass of red wine. Pours herself another. She made soup earlier, she says. Heats it up, puts out homemade bread, and asks Dorea to set the table.

They are both silent as they prepare the meal.

There is a knock on the door and a nurse enters. Elpida greets her and talks to her in Greek. The nurse climbs the stairs.

We eat the vegetable soup and the bread.

Elpida asks about my journey and for how long I am staying.

I tell her that I am intending to stay for a week.

She says we will talk more tomorrow. Now we need to do

ordinary things. Eat food, have a bath and go to bed. Tomorrow we will know more.

I walk the few steps down to the Hotel Miranda. I follow Elpida's advice and have a bath. I make sure it is very hot.

I try to sleep, but high voltages of electricity run through my body. I drift in and out of a delirious sleep.

I hear Garrick laugh. Then the laughter stops and he shouts, "Keep swimming!"

Jacques

Hydra, Greece, Thanksgiving 2018

It is Saturday.

I have breakfast at the hotel, go for a walk down the harbor, have another espresso. It's my third, and it's only 8:30am. Elpida said I could visit around 10am.

I should go for a walk, explore the town, but I am not able to focus. I am feverish. One minute shivering with cold, the next burning up. My feet feel fuzzy, my whole body feels strange and I am shaking, quivering. I want to sit down somewhere and feel safe.

There is nobody in the cafe. It's freezing and the locals are having breakfast at home. No tourists either.

I am fidgety. My laptop is on the table. The only thing that helps me keep it together while I wait is typing words. I put my shoulder bag on my lap. A book falls out and on to the floor. I pick it up. *And There Was Light*, the book that came with Garrick's parcel. I was not going to take it with me. But I saw it lying on the living room table as I was leaving Jakob's house, and I didn't want him to find it. He makes sarcastic remarks of all things spiritual.

I don't want to read this book. I avoided it the whole journey. On the plane, I read all the flight magazines, and watched a movie, and on the boat I stared at the sea. I should leave the book here in the cafe. I don't want to carry around its dead weight anymore. I put it on the table next to mine. I look away, drink my coffee. Then the young waitress comes over and asks if it is my book. She smiles and puts it down on my table, and leaves.

I think about taking the book to the bathroom and leaving it there, but instead I open it randomly.

Jacques is ready, and he quickly informs me that he saw

fever as a way for his body to eliminate poison, and not just the physical kind.

I am shaking with cold as I read his words. My vision blurs. I'm in a muddle.

He goes on saying it was emotions which caused his body to erupt, and that he soon stopped caring about the origin of the fever, because what mattered was that he was being broken open and taken over from the inside.

Oh, I get this Jacques, believe me… because I am being taken over right now, from head to foot and asked to surrender... and instead I am fighting... with my steel body and tight fists. How about that, Jacques?

I put the book back in my bag.

Jacques.

Why are you still pestering me?

What do you want?

You are dead.

Stay dead.

The Fisherman

Hydra, Greece, Thanksgiving 2018

I sit in Elpida's kitchen again. I ask for tea when she offers coffee. I say I am sick, I have a fever. She gets paracetamol from a cupboard, and I swallow two white pills with my tea.

"I just washed him. Nurse cares during the week. I do weekends. He'd do this for me," Elpida says. She looks tired.

"He painted in studio every day until lunch. Then, fishing or back to painting. All afternoon."

Dorea enters and says a bright, "Hi!". She gets an apple from the fridge and walks out again.

"He fished Dorea out of sea," Elpida says, looking straight at me. "Eleven years ago. Will be twelve next week."

I have no words.

"Erik visited Aris, friend on Lesbos, selling art. They went with fishing boat. The friend always pull up bodies. Refugees. Erik started, too. Then could not stay away. Always pulling people out of the sea and painting faces," Elpida says. "Twelve years ago Erik pulled woman up from sea. Alone. Pregnant. They took her to Aris' house… Woman died, Dorea born… Erik cut the cord." Elpida mimics a scissors gesture. "Brought child to me. Tiny sea creature on my kitchen table."

I am looking at her and I tremble with cold. I cannot talk, so I stay quiet. She knows I am drinking her words.

"We did not report baby for long time…government bad with refugees sometimes... smashing their boats... people drowning in the sea... every night."

She goes towards the fridge. Gets one of the magnets. It's a photo. "See? … Dorea, three months old."

I look at a tiny baby in a small basket. The serious dark eyes are gazing straight into the camera.

"Many people from the islands help refugees," Elpida says. "Greek fishermen save refugees from the sea for years."

So cold, so cold. I ask for a blanket. I am shivering. My teeth are clattering. Elpida pours me another cup of tea.

"Ginger tea," she says. "Warm you up." Then she wraps a soft, purple woolen blanket around me.

My hands cling to the hot, blue ceramic cup. My nose is running and Elpida passes me a tissue.

I think about Dorea, that she is lucky to have Elpida as her mother.

"They come to Lesbos, Samos, Chios from Iraq, Afghanistan, Syria, Somalia," she continues. "Thousands of them. Hundred thousands in the last ten years. And so many dead at sea."

I sip my tea. Turn to look at a cheerful painting showing sunshine, flowers and a rainbow.

"Only Dorea's paintings in the kitchen," Elpida says in response to my gaze.

"I told him no sea work in here. This is free zone. We feed our lives and souls here."

She has done well, I am thinking. This kitchen is a good place to sit. It has warmth, colors, life. Her warmth.

"He stayed with Aris on Lesbos many weeks. Came back with ferry boat. Too far to go with fishing boat. At home, he painted like crazy. Then, returned to Lesbos."

"He got obsessed. Disappeared from me. The sea brought me a child, but took husband... I fight with him to keep him back. He not well at sea."

She shifts her position several times as she tells me this. Her eyes are avoiding mine.

"The coastguard cannot cover all the sea. 'People are dying while I make useless art,' he shouted when I begged for him to stay at home... He screamed in his sleep, 'Women and children first!'. Woke up Dorea... After fishing up the dead, he shut himself in studio and not come out. I brought him food. He slept on dirty couch, and when better he came home with croissants or flowers... Not easy on the child," she says and falls silent.

My shivering has turned into fire, and I am burning up. I remove the blanket. I can see that her words have not run out, so I wait.

"Adoption took a long time... and so many are orphans here..." She strokes Dorea's photo. "Some people, fishermen, are racist. Don't want refugees. Don't want them in Greece. Many times Erik and Aris saw fishermen with big boats. They laughed at refugees in trouble."

"On Hydra, not many refugees. Tourists. But some people shout at us in the streets... children shout at Dorea at school..."

"Last week a friend found a woman. Her body on the shore. On island not far from here. He said needs a doctor for his mind. Cannot see these bodies any more. 'We are guilty when something goes wrong. We have to do something,' he said... Erik felt the same. His responsibility to do something. 'They are not just names', he repeated to Dorea and me. '...the ones that don't make it... calling out... Someone must give them voice. I can only paint them. The world must listen, see, look.'

"He sat with Dorea. From when she was four years old, he made her write. He told her it was like fishing. She learned. He made her write about things around her, feelings too... They read books and poems... and they read Dorea's writings to me, and that is how we made our family. He said to Dorea that he was just a fisherman. But he knew how to fill spaces with movement, light. He wished for her to fill space with words. Become a famous writer. Dora loved this, wanted his attention."

The words are finished. The kitchen seems different. The stories have painted pictures, which are still hanging in the air.

She looks at me and asks how I am.

I say I am burning up.

She tells me I can see Erik if I want to.

I sit on the chair next to him again. Look around the room.

His face is pale. Today my hands are warmer than his. I touch him and hope I will not pass on my fever.

I am expecting Dorea to join me, but she is not coming. I need her to fill the room with her words, her reading.

I feel the weight of my bag leaning against my leg. The same book that I read for Mom when I sat by her bed is in that bag.

I do the obvious.

I open it randomly, and Jacques' voice softly fills the space. He tells Erik that he doesn't want to recount the story of his life, because the only thing worth telling now is his reason for loving life. That is the one real subject, he says.

I pause.

Erik doesn't need those words… It was clear from Elpida's stories that he loved life. That's why he could not stop pulling people out of the sea.

I am not reading for him.

The words are for me.

I look at the painting on the wall across from the bed. It is the sea again.

Not the dark sea. A bright sea, with a sunrise. I stand up and walk towards it.

I study the yellow, white, golden, blue. There is an inscription on the bottom-right corner: *This is all he asks of you, that you live and respond to his grace in the here and now.*

I start shivering again and close the window. This room is like a fridge.

I go back and sit on the chair. I look at Erik to see if he has noticed my presence. I search for a sign telling me he has been listening. It seems foolish to keep reading. But I want him to hear my voice. Want it to go inside him, have an effect.

I don't know what I can say to him. Despite all the words, I am mute.

So I let Jacques speak for me again.

I hear him say that he always felt safe, and that although he couldn't see, he trusted that the trees he climbed would hold him, and the paths he walked would take him home. He says that there only is one story, the story of life.

Then I don't want to read any more. I sit next to the bed. I am feeling floaty and cold and thirsty. I drink the water left on Erik's bedside table. I find it hard to leave.

I put Jacques' book back in my bag, and search for the paracetamols. Instead my hand grabs the laptop. I pull it out, open it on my thighs. I sit in silence. Stare at Erik.

Then I clear my throat and start to read the lines of dry, black, stick-bodied letters:

For three months now, instead of studying for my exams, I have been sitting at my white desk, alternating between staring at the ghostly landscape outside and sifting through the words of a twelve-year-old me.

Now that the words are here, they fill the space and crowd my head as I look out of the window. The snow is black. It was pure and soft, and now it is hard, dirty and icy. I know that this grainy, black snow will line the streets outside for many months. Slowly, I will forget that warmth and sun and spring are possible. Every year, I forget. And then suddenly, as if out of nowhere, the ice will melt, the mud will stick to my shoes, and new life will be revealed. You should know this, as you grew up here as well. Or have you forgotten what it is like when the sun goes away for months on end, and the short glimmer of light at noon is too weak to carry the slightest hope of spring?

Dorea opens the door. She pulls the stool next to mine and leans against me.

We sit together without talking. She takes my right hand in her two hands.

We don't speak the same language. She smiles at me, says, "Sister."

She waits for my response. I am not giving her one. I was reading my story for Erik. I don't care whether he understands. Now I want him to have my story. I look at Dorea, who is smiling up at me. I feel angry. She is interrupting. She is listening intently, like an animal, penetrating my boundaries with her presence. She says something in Greek. I look at her, not sure what she wants from me. A big sister. I don't think so.

I feel her insistence, like a shark following the smell of blood. I am hiding. She is waiting. I am running. She is following. Now she sings a slow Greek song, holding my hand, not looking at me with her eyes, but with all the eyes of her body. Her singing is a sharp hook, has a bait. It sinks deep into my dark waters. Shimmers, gleams. Tempting the forgotten. I look away. I stare at the wall. She is singing. I get up, open the windows. The breeze is cold. The sea is dark. I wait. She sings. I wait some more. I go back to my seat. She stops singing. We sit in silence. She is still listening, but turned away. Rejected. Hurt. We are both looking away. I stare at Erik's painting of the sea.

We sit without speaking or looking at each other. For a long time, we sit there, without looking. Then she stands up. I know she is going to leave. She walks towards the door. And I become aware of a slight movement happening deep, deep down in a dark, forgotten lake inside me. The tiniest fish has jumped. It is minuscule. Without substance. Ghostly. Spreading almost invisible rings. Revealing that something has stirred. Is moving. Towards the gleaming hook. Something shy. Far away. Shadowy thin. Is swimming towards her. The line is slack now. She is not pulling. But the shy is jumping... into my hands.

My hands; hot, burning hands. Not white. Not toads. Not lizards. Red blood pulsing. My reptile hands becoming human hands. I know these hands. They know me. I am these hands. I am these arms. I am these legs. These breasts, this neck, this face. My face. My eyes. I turn and look at Dorea. Reach out and say her name. My eyes and her eyes. We stay like that. My arm stretched out. Her body twisted, half towards me, half towards the door. The space between us frozen. No breath. She looks away. Then she breathes in. She breathes out. And she moves towards me. I breathe out. She takes my hand. I sink down on the chair. Pull her gently on to my lap. Her body is tense. I feel her heart beating fast. I sniff her hair. She relaxes, gets heavier. Her left shoulder is burrowing into my chest. She smells of cinnamon and salt sea. I put my arms tightly around her. I hear a familiar laugh. Garrick. Like a beep in my ear.

The air becomes thick like water. Golden, liquid light.

We lean forward into it, and it carries us.

It holds us and moves us.

It is in us and around us, and we swim-fly in it together.

The laptop is resting on the bedside table. Lines of black words. I look at Erik. I look at Dorea. I grab the laptop, and watch my human hands hit "Select All," and I see the black letters submerged by blue.

My cockroach shell dissolves, liquefies.

I press DELETE.

White screen, like fresh, luminous snow.

Acknowledgments

I would like to thank Dominic James and everyone else at JHS for their trust and their kind publishing practices. I am grateful to Kerry Keeler and Elizabeth Oakes for providing me with a beautiful place to write, from where I could hear and smell the waves of the Pacific Ocean. I am deeply appreciative of my friend Lucy for her teaching and guidance in the tradition of the lineage of The Common Life, and I express my gratitude to Rudy Bauer of the Washington Center for Consciousness Studies. A loving "Thank you" goes to my husband, Stefano, for the care he took in helping to bring out the essence and light of Luna's voice. And of course I am deeply thankful to my dear friend Michael Cogan: without his consistent encouragement, wisdom and kindness, this book would never have found its way into the world.

Author's Note

Luna reads from the wonderful book *And There Was Light by* Jacques Lusseyran, Parabola Books Edition, 1987.

The song Geraldine sings at the talent show, *The Caravan to the Land of Plenty,* was loosely inspired by Willie Nelson's song *Living in the Promised Land.*

Put simply, we publish great stories. Whether it's literary or popular, a gentle tale or a pulsating thriller, the connecting theme in all Roundfire fiction titles is that once you pick them up you won't want to put them down.

If you have enjoyed this book, why not tell other readers by posting a review on your preferred book site.

Recent bestsellers from Roundfire are:

The Bookseller's Sonnets

Andi Rosenthal

The Bookseller's Sonnets intertwines three love stories with a tale of religious identity and mystery spanning five hundred years and three countries.

Paperback: 978-1-84694-342-3 ebook: 978-184694-626-4

Birds of the Nile

An Egyptian Adventure

N.E. David

Ex-diplomat Michael Blake wanted a quiet birding trip up the Nile – he wasn't expecting a revolution.

Paperback: 978-1-78279-158-4 ebook: 978-1-78279-157-7

Blood Profit$

The Lithium Conspiracy

J. Victor Tomaszek, James N. Patrick, Sr.

The blood of the many for the profits of the few… *Blood Profit$* will take you into the cigar-smoke-filled room where American policy and laws are really made.

Paperback: 978-1-78279-483-7 ebook: 978-1-78279-277-2

The Burden

A Family Saga

N.E. David

Frank will do anything to keep his mother and father apart. But he's carrying baggage – and it might just weigh him down ...

Paperback: 978-1-78279-936-8 ebook: 978-1-78279-937-5

The Cause

Roderick Vincent

The second American Revolution will be a fire lit from an internal spark.

Paperback: 978-1-78279-763-0 ebook: 978-1-78279-762-3

Don't Drink and Fly

The Story of Bernice O'Hanlon: Part One

Cathie Devitt

Bernice is a witch living in Glasgow. She loses her way in her life and wanders off the beaten track looking for the garden of enlightenment.

Paperback: 978-1-78279-016-7 ebook: 978-1-78279-015-0

Gag

Melissa Unger

One rainy afternoon in a Brooklyn diner, Peter Howland punctures an egg with his fork. Repulsed, Peter pushes the plate away and never eats again.

Paperback: 978-1-78279-564-3 ebook: 978-1-78279-563-6

The Master Yeshua

The Undiscovered Gospel of Joseph

Joyce Luck

Jesus is not who you think he is. The year is 75 CE. Joseph ben Jude is frail and ailing, but he has a prophecy to fulfil …

Paperback: 978-1-78279-974-0 ebook: 978-1-78279-975-7

On the Far Side, There's a Boy

Paula Coston

Martine Haslett, a thirty-something 1980s woman, plays hard on the fringes of the London drag club scene until one night which prompts her to sign up to a charity. She writes to a young Sri Lankan boy, with consequences far and long.

Paperback: 978-1-78279-574-2 ebook: 978-1-78279-573-5

Tuareg

Alberto Vazquez-Figueroa

With over 5 million copies sold worldwide, Tuareg is a classic adventure story from best-selling author Alberto Vazquez-Figueroa, about honour, revenge and a clash of cultures.

Paperback: 978-1-84694-192-4

Readers of ebooks can buy or view any of these bestsellers by clicking on the live link in the title. Most titles are published in paperback and as an ebook. Paperbacks are available in traditional bookshops. Both print and ebook formats are available online.

Find more titles and sign up to our readers' newsletter at http://www.johnhuntpublishing.com/fiction

Follow us on Facebook at https://www.facebook.com/JHPfiction and Twitter at https://twitter.com/JHPFiction